THE
NEED

Center Point
Large Print

**This Large Print Book carries the
Seal of Approval of N.A.V.H.**

THE NEED

— A NOVEL —

HELEN PHILLIPS

CENTER POINT LARGE PRINT
THORNDIKE, MAINE

This book is for my mother,
Susan Zimmermann,
and for my sister,
Katherine Rose Phillips,
September 2, 1979–July 29, 2012

Statements that happen at the same time

In different places, at different times
In the same place, at different times
In different places form a single score.
—**GEOFFREY G. O'BRIEN,** "Fidelio"

We stood facing each other the way, when you come upon a deer unexpectedly, you both freeze for a moment, mutually startled, and in that exchange there seems to be but one glance, as if you and the other are sharing the same pair of eyes.
—**MARY RUEFLE,** "My Private Property"

Tennyson said that if we could but understand a single flower we might know who we are and what the world is. Perhaps he was trying to say that there is nothing, however humble, that does not imply the history of the world and its infinite concatenation of causes and effects.
—**JORGE LUIS BORGES,** "The Zahir"

— PART 1 —

1

She crouched in front of the mirror in the dark, clinging to them. The baby in her right arm, the child in her left.

There were footsteps in the other room.

She had heard them an instant ago. She had switched off the light, scooped up her son, pulled her daughter across the bedroom to hide in the far corner.

She had heard footsteps.

But she was sometimes hearing things. A passing ambulance mistaken for Ben's nighttime wail. The moaning hinges of the bathroom cabinet mistaken for Viv's impatient pre-tantrum sigh.

Her heart and blood were loud. She needed them to not be so loud.

Another step.

Or was it a soft hiccup from Ben? Or was it her own knee joint cracking beneath thirty-six pounds of Viv?

She guessed the intruder was in the middle of the living room now, halfway to the bedroom.

She knew there was no intruder.

Viv smiled at her in the feeble light of the faraway streetlamp. Viv always craved games that were slightly frightening. Any second now, she would demand the next move in this wondrous new one.

Her desperation for her children's silence manifested as a suffocating force, the desire for a pillow, a pair of thick socks, anything she could shove into them to perfect their muteness and save their lives.

Another step. Hesitant, but undeniable.

Or maybe not.

Ben was drowsy, tranquil, his thumb in his mouth.

Viv was looking at her with curious, cunning eyes.

David was on a plane somewhere over another continent.

The babysitter had marched off to get a Friday-night beer with her girls.

Could she squeeze the children under the bed and go out to confront the intruder on her own? Could she press them into the closet, keep them safe among her shoes?

Her phone was in the other room, in her bag, dropped and forgotten by the front door when she arrived home from work twenty-five minutes ago to a blueberry-stained Ben, to Viv parading through the living room chanting "Birth-Day! Birth-Day!" with an uncapped purple marker held aloft in her right hand like the Statue of Liberty's torch.

"Viv!" she had roared when the marker grazed the white wall of the hallway as her daughter ran toward her. But to no avail: a purple scar to join the others, the green crayon, the red pencil.

A Friday-night beer with my girls.

How exotic, she had thought distantly, handing over the wad of cash. Erika was twenty-three, and buoyant, and brave. She had wanted, above all else, someone brave to look after the children.

"Now what?" Viv said, starting to strain against her arm. Thankfully, a stage whisper rather than a shriek.

But even so the footsteps shifted direction, toward the bedroom.

If David were home, in the basement, practicing, she would be stomping their code on the floor, five times for *Come up right this second,* usually because both kids needed everything from her at once.

A step, a step?

This problem of hers had begun about four years ago, soon after Viv's birth. She confessed it only to David, wanting to know if he ever experienced the same sensation, trying and failing to capture it in words: the minor disorientations that sometimes plagued her, the small errors of eyes and ears. The conviction that the rumble underfoot was due to an earthquake rather than a garbage truck. The conviction that there was something somehow *off* about a piece of litter found amid the fossils in the Pit at work. A brief flash or dizziness that, for a millisecond, caused reality to shimmer or waver or disintegrate slightly. In those instants, her best recourse was to steady her body against something solid— David, if he happened to be nearby, or a table, a tree, or the dirt wall of the Pit—until the world resettled into known patterns and she could once more move invincible, unshakable, through her day.

Yes, David said whenever she brought it up; he knew what she meant, kind of. His diagnosis: sleep deprivation and/or dehydration.

Viv squirmed out of her grasp. She was a slippery kid, and, with only one arm free, there was no way Molly could prevent her daughter's escape.

"Stay. Right. Here," she mouthed with all the intensity she could infuse into a voiceless command.

But Viv tiptoed theatrically toward the bedroom door, which was open just a crack, and grinned back at her mother, the grin turned grimace by the eerie light of the streetlamp.

Molly didn't know whether to move or stay put. Any quick action—a hurl across the room, a seizure of the T-shirt—was sure to unleash a scream or a laugh from Viv, was sure to disrupt

14

Ben, lulled nearly to sleep by the panicked bouncing of Molly's arm.

Viv pulled the door open.

Molly had never before noticed that the bedroom door squeaked, a sound that now seemed intolerably loud.

It would be so funny to tell David about this when he landed.

I turned off the light and made the kids hide in the corner of the bedroom. I was totally petrified. And it was nothing!

Beneath the hilarity would lie her secret concern about this little problem of hers. But their laughter would neutralize it, almost.

She listened hard for the footsteps. There were none.

She stood up. She raised Ben's limp, snoozing body to her chest. She flicked the light back on. The room looked warm. Orderly. The gray quilt tucked tight at the corners. She would make mac and cheese. She would thaw some peas. She stepped toward the doorway, where Viv stood still, peering out.

"Who's that guy?" Viv said.

2

Eight hours before she heard the footsteps in the other room, she was at the Phillips 66 fossil quarry, at the bottom of the Pit, chiseling away at the grayish rock.

She had been looking forward to it, an hour alone in the Pit, the absorption into the endless quest for fossils, the stark solitude of it, thirty yards removed from the defunct gas station, away from the ever-increasing hubbub about the Bible, away from the phone calls and emails and hate mail, away from the impatient reporters and scornful hoaxers and zealots swiftly emerging from the woodwork.

"Almost a decade of mind-bending plant-fossil finds, a bunch of them *unplaceable based on our current understanding of the fossil record,*" Corey had griped last week, "and no one but us and a handful of other paleobotany dorks gave a damn about this site until now."

As Molly stood in the Pit, her focus eluded her, the obsessive focus that had been the trademark of her working life, the longtime source of mockery and admiration from her colleagues and her husband alike. *Your freak focus,* David called it.

Now, though, she was just outrageously tired: soggy logic, fuzzy vision. It was inconceivable that in forty-five minutes she would be standing in front of a tour group, saying things.

The night prior, Ben had awoken every hour or so to howl for a few moments before dropping back into silence. Again and again she almost went to him. Finally, at 3:34 a.m., she entered the children's room to find him standing naked in the crib, gripping the wooden bars. He had somehow managed to remove his red footed pajamas by himself, a skill she would have guessed was still months off. When he saw her, he stopped shrieking and smiled proudly.

"Good for you," she whispered, nauseated with exhaustion.

She lifted him out of the crib, anxious about the possibility of waking Viv, and sank down into the rocking chair to nurse him. She shouldn't do it. It was bad for his freshly grown teeth to have milk on them at night. He was too old for night nursing. But in the dark, disoriented, she sometimes gave in, less to his nagging and more to her own desire to hold a person close and, effortlessly, give him what he most wanted.

Yet tonight, for the first time ever, he didn't want to nurse. Instead, he pressed his head against her clavicle and then patted her cheek four times before leaning away from her, leaning back toward the crib.

"Shouldn't we put your pajamas on?"

He was woozy, though, already almost asleep again, and anyway the radiator was going too strong for this uncannily warm early spring, so she returned him to the crib in just his diaper.

She had finally fallen back to sleep in her own bed when there was a mouth an inch from her face.

"I'm carrying a tree."

"What?"

"I'm *carrying* a *tree.*"

"You're carrying a tree?"

"No! Not a tree, a *dream!*"

"You're carrying a dream?"

"*No!* I-HAD-A-SCARY-DREAM."

She and David had a running joke about how they both feared their kids at night the same way that, as children, they'd feared monsters under the bed. Beasts that would rise up from the side of your bed, seize you with sharp nails and demand things of you.

She shouldn't do it, but she did: hauled Viv into bed, parked the kid between her body and David's, which slumbered through everything, even through Viv's sleep dance, her spread eagle evolving into pirouette evolving into breaststroke, her almost-four years swelling to take up far more space in the bed than their combined sixty-eight.

So you wake up ill with tiredness but it's your own fault for not being better, stricter. So you stand there at work wondering what you have to offer the world, just your strained, drained body and your weakness. But somehow you crouch down again, again you hack at the unyielding earth.

And that was when she saw it.

That unmistakable brightness, the warm color of childhood, a wish in water.

A penny, lodged deep in the dirt at the bottom of the Pit.

A new penny, that glow of the recently minted.

So, the most current artifact of the five to date: the Coca-Cola bottle, the toy soldier, the Altoids tin, the potsherd, the Bible. Her strange discoveries had taken place gradually, over the course of the past nine months, starting with the Coca-Cola bottle her first week back at work after Ben's birth (she had picked it up, tilted her head this way and that, trying to figure out whether the oddity lay in her or in the font). Just the tiniest dribble of random objects amid the tsunami of plant fossils. But, here, another find, only a month after the Bible.

As she photographed the penny and recorded its GPS coordinates (hoping her own stupid footsteps hadn't already altered its location), adrenaline blasted through her fatigue. She ought to leave it in situ and call Shaina to find out how soon she could drive across town to come take a look. Shaina was the first person Molly had contacted when she found the Coca-Cola bottle, needing the archaeologist perspective from her old grad-school friend. But from the start Shaina had taken a dubious stance on the objects: she complained that Molly and Corey and Roz, all with their typical paleobotanist's disregard for the maintenance of the stratigraphy, had long ago made any meaningful archaeological analysis very nearly impossible. "You work by way of sledgehammer," Shaina had said. "I work by way of sieve."

"But you think the Bible was really printed in the early 1900s?"

"Look," Shaina had said over beers at the nearest bar, "for all I know, some high-tech prankster buried that Bible in the Pit hours before you uncovered it."

"And the others?" Molly pressed.

"Same. Sure, like, with the potsherd: yes, interesting, it's not a pattern I've ever seen before. But it's so small, and with no organic material found nearby that I could use to confidently carbon-date it . . . Yes, sure, I'm weirded out by an old Altoids tin that's slightly the wrong shape. Yes, I'd like to identify somewhere, sometime, another plastic toy soldier that was manufactured with a monkey tail. I'll study them a bit more because I can tell you care a lot. But there's just not really enough to work with."

The penny glinted up at Molly. She and it, alone together. This was what had drawn her to a field that involved unveiling the layers of the earth, unsure what you were seeking: this throb of fascination. She used the tip of her trowel to dislodge the penny.

"Excuse me," she said to the penny as she pried it out. Minted this year, she noted as she slid it into a baggie from her pocket. She would postpone any further examination until she was back in the lab. She wanted to pause here, between not-knowing and knowing. She looked up: above her, beyond the twenty-foot walls of the Pit, the sky was the color of milk.

3

She had no choice but to look out into the living room herself.

What could she do to make sure he would shoot her and spare the children?

"Did you really see a man?" she whispered.

Viv smiled up at her.

"Move," Molly said, trying to scoot her daughter out of the doorway with her hip.

But Viv, sensing her mother's urgency, tensed her muscles and refused to budge.

"Viv," she said, suddenly nonchalant, "go on out to the living room. I'm putting B down on my bed and you can't bother him while he sleeps."

That was all it took. Viv let go of the doorjamb, jumped onto the bed beside her brother, began harassing him with coos and kisses.

The ploy bought Molly perhaps forty-five seconds before the baby woke or the big sister tired of the provocation. She hurried to the doorway. A peculiar half laugh rose in her: hurrying to see who had broken into their home, just as she was always hurrying to get ready for work, hurrying to put the groceries away, hurrying to take a shit, every single thing in life shoved between the needs of a pair of people who weighed a cumulative fifty-seven pounds.

Who's that guy?

But as she looked out at the living room, she saw only its normal end-of-day chaos, a scattering of Cheerios, a ruin of blocks, the crayons splayed like many fingers pointing. Usually the sight would have wearied her, but at this moment, colored by her relief, it seemed terribly beautiful.

It was an open, spare room—no place to hide. Just couch, bookshelves, chairs, dining table. The only possible hiding spot—as she'd learned last month when, for an entire weekend, Viv refused to do anything except play hide-and-seek—was inside the squat, ugly coffee table that doubled as an enormous toy box. It had been so coffin-like in there that she had begun to miss them fiercely when she heard their voices, their footsteps (David's surprisingly heavy for such a skinny man; Viv's quick, frantic; Ben's so dainty, halting and sticky), moving through the rooms as they searched for her. But no casual intruder would realize the coffee table was hollow inside.

Everything was fine, fine, fine.

She strode to the kitchen. Turned on the overhead. Opened the freezer to pull out the peas.

In the bedroom, Viv screamed.

4

Her makeshift office was at the back of the gas-station-turned-research-lab-and-display-room, in what had once been the candy aisle of the Phillips 66. She pulled her wallet from her bag, unzipped the overstuffed change purse, was lucky enough to find a penny also minted in the current year.

She placed the penny from her wallet on an examination tray. She had never in her life looked so closely at a penny. The phone on her desk was ringing but she ignored it. She tugged open the plastic baggie, shook the penny from the Pit out onto the examination tray along with a sprinkle of Pit dust, and wrote beneath the penny on the left *CONTROL* and beneath the one on the right *PIT.*

What would it be this time? A president other than Lincoln? Or the profile of a leader unknown to her? The word *PEACE* or *ORDER* rather than the word *LIBERTY?* A sunburst instead of a shield? An alphabet she didn't recognize? Or, more likely, some subtle shift of typography or proportion barely perceptible even to her eye trained in tracing the faintest veins of ancient leaves.

24

Just then her milk came down. It often came at moments of high emotion. That slight ache or buzz, valves pressured into opening, the simultaneous relief and frustration, her bra damp in two focused spots. Reminder: Mother. Reminder: Animal.

Her breast pump was somewhere in the darkness beneath the old metal desk. When had she last rinsed the shields and the valves? It was a hassle to clean them. She would need to scrub them before pumping. If she were more on top of things, she would have taken them home to boil them in hot water for five minutes.

But for now: the two pennies, side by side. Mundane and sacred at the same time. She thought of her children.

The penny from the Pit. Heads side: above Lincoln's profile, the words *IN GOD WE TRUST.* To the left of his profile, the word *LIBERTY.* To the right, the current year.

She searched for a difference in Abe's facial expression; was he perhaps a tad more wry, a tad less stern, in the penny from the Pit?

But eventually she had to admit that the penny from the Pit was identical to the penny from her wallet. The difference would lie, perhaps, on the other side.

Her bra damper by the second.

Because her fingers were quivering, it took two tries before she managed to flip over the coin from her wallet, three tries for the coin from the Pit.

Tails: beneath the declaration *UNITED STATES OF AMERICA,* a shield emblazoned at the top with the phrase *E PLURIBUS UNUM,* and, on a banner in front of the shield, the words *ONE CENT.*

On both, the shields were the same shape, each bearing thirteen stripes. Beneath the shields, the same miniscule *LB* on the left-hand side and *JFM* on the right-hand side.

Two identical pennies.

She felt ridiculous. So she or Corey or Roz had accidentally dropped a penny at the bottom of the Pit. So what.

She picked up both pennies and put them in her wallet.

The burden of the milk.

Her fatigue returned like a hand pressing down on her skull.

5

There was almost no time between the instant she heard the scream and the instant she was back in the bedroom. Yet it was more than enough time for the image: their small bodies, their blood on the gray quilt, their eyes four huge hurting questions. How could she be so stupid, she'd done the idiotic horror-movie thing, leaving the vulnerable flank unguarded while bumbling about in search of the threat.

But in the bedroom there was no blood.

There was just a baby sleeping on the bed and a kid jumping up and down beside him, grabbing her crotch and anxiously apologizing: "I'm sorry I peed on your bed!"

Usually she would have chided Viv for jumping so close to the baby, for ignoring her fifteen minutes earlier when Molly had asked if she needed to pee, for the unnecessarily alarming scream. Instead, she seized her, airlifted her to the bathroom, used the situation as an excuse to hold her daughter closer than close. She grabbed the potty insert and plopped Viv down on the toilet and yanked off her urine-soaked pants and undies.

"Why are you crying?" Viv said.

In the bedroom, Ben began to cry.

6

Never mind Corey's touching touches (the potpourri, the lemon soap, the wrought-iron tissue box): a convenience store bathroom is a convenience store bathroom. It was one of those faucets that would run for only ten seconds before turning itself off. She did the best she could, then held the pump parts beneath the hand dryer mounted to the wall. She returned to her office, pulled closed the curtain that served as a door, unbuttoned her shirt, unfastened the cups of her nursing bra, inserted the tubes into the shields, hooked herself up to the machine, turned the dial to its highest setting.

Viv had covered her face in horror the first time she witnessed her mother pumping milk for her brother. "What it doing to you?" she said, staring at the machine through her fingers, at her mother's nipples extending and retracting, misshapen by the plastic funnels.

But Viv had since grown accustomed to it, its distinctive wheeze, and came to consider it a sort of pet. She would sit beside her mother on the couch, matching her breathing to the breathing of the pump, hyperventilating along with it, stroking the pump with one hand as though her presence was somehow facilitating the process.

Here, now, in Molly's office, the milk was not coming, not quickly enough. A drop from the right, two drops from the left. She needed at least three ounces from each. And after that, she needed to deliver the milk to the minifridge and transform from one kind of person into another, pull herself back together before the tour—which, if the past two and a half weeks were any indication, would be larger than the previous day's.

She thought, with longing, of the time—it already seemed so distant—when the daily tour consisted of just a handful of paleobotany amateurs or foreign tourists. On the fateful day, less than a month ago, when she had brought the Bible out from her office at the end of the tour to show it off, there were just three people in her tour group, a kindly Brazilian couple and an elderly paleo enthusiast. Perhaps it was a slight act of defiance, after Shaina's and Roz's and Corey's overall dismissive attitudes toward her nonfossil finds ("Molly's little litter," Corey dubbed it; "H-O-A-X," Roz spelled dryly). Or perhaps it was just that they had somehow clicked, their tiny tour group; the Q and A had gone on for forty-five minutes longer than usual, and when the wife asked if they'd ever found anything in the Pit aside from plant fossils, Molly had felt safe, open, eager to share this incredible thing.

Molly assumed it was the elderly paleo enthusiast who had called the local paper; anyway, there was a reporter on the tour the next day.

Still the milk would not come. Every time she pumped she felt sorry for cows. When she poured cow's milk for Viv she experienced a flash of mother-to-mother gratitude: *Thank you, Ma Cow, for letting me steal your milk for my own offspring.*

She looked up at the drop ceiling with its uneven tiles, marveled yet again that the Phillips 66 retained its gas-station smell even now, that eternal mix of Jolly Rancher and beef jerky, the scent of quarry dust just a thin overlay. She waited impatiently for the milk to flow. But the more impatient you were, the more the milk resisted the pump.

She thought again of the twin pennies. Stalwart, insignificant.

The milk gushed into the bottles.

7

She ran into the bedroom, where Ben—crying—had flipped himself over and crawled toward the bottom of the bed. She caught him right as he tumbled off. She could have felt victorious for the improbable save, but instead she just felt guilty for having left him alone on the bed when she knew better than anyone how mobile he had become, how swift.

Yet there was little opportunity to indulge her guilt, to reflect upon it and make resolutions for the future, because in the bathroom Viv was calling for her, and Ben was clawing affectionately at her neck (she needed to trim his nails, she'd been meaning to do it for days, but he guarded them so ferociously whenever she brought out the clippers), and her heart rate was elevated as it always was when she was the sole caretaker of her children, imaginary footsteps or no. She wondered if other mothers experienced it, this permanent state of mild panic, and worried that perhaps they didn't, that perhaps there was something wrong with her. What a phenomenon it was to be with her children, to spend every moment so acutely aware of the abyss, the potential injury flickering within each second.

Ben now kissing her neck, but he was still learning what a kiss was, so his consisted of a wide-open mouth and drool and teeth.

Viv now delivering a litany from her toilet perch: "Can you please read me *Statue of Liberty*? Wait, no, actually, can you please read me *Birthday Blue*? No, actually, really, can you please read me *The Why Book*?"

Moment by moment, maddened by them and melted by them, maddened/melted, maddened/melted, maddened/melted.

She relished the unpleasant kiss. She said to Viv, "Okay, okay, okay—wait, I still don't know where *The Why Book* is, did you and Erika find it?" She stepped out of the bedroom and walked to the bathroom, just a few steps. If she hadn't been passing through the hall at that exact instant, she would have missed it: the lid of the coffee-table-toy-chest lifting up a centimeter and then immediately, gently, sinking back down.

8

It was with some pride that she screwed the tops onto the bottles of milk. Nearly four ounces in each. She pressed the pair of bottles, warm with her milk, against her cheeks. Partway the accomplishment of an animal, partway the accomplishment of a deity. Then she zipped the bottles into the small cloth cooler where she hid them; perhaps Corey and Roz would prefer not to see her bodily juices sitting beside their lunches in the communal fridge.

She rehooked, rebuttoned.

A couple of weeks back she had put a photograph of the kids as the wallpaper on her computer; they were wearing backpacks too large for their frames and hugging each other too tightly. Neither was smiling. They seemed scared, big-eyed. It was just the chance of the shot, the millisecond of solemnity caught by her phone's camera amid shrieks of laughter, yet it struck her, almost pained her, to see them so vulnerable. She hadn't realized how frightened they looked until she saw the picture on the larger screen. She reminded herself for perhaps the twentieth time to change the image. But not now. Later, when she had time. Ha.

On her way from her office to the improvised kitchen, repurposed from the beer and slushy section of the gas station, she almost collided with Corey, who was carrying a pile of mail. He was wearing his *I Put the Pal in Paleobotany* T-shirt, a custom-ordered gift from Roz. She had gotten three, one for each of them. The exact kind of thoughtful act that people with young children don't have time to execute. Molly's resided at the bottom of her pajama drawer, but Corey, somehow, managed to pull it off.

"Your fault," he said, theatrically waving the mail in her face. "Roz and I just want to sit around wondering about prehistoric plants."

She recognized the handwritten, crooked-stamp quality of hate mail, and the dread of the past few weeks, the shock of something so quiet and private going viral, getting out of control, settled dense in her stomach after her morning of ignoring it.

"I'm sorry," she said. It *was* her fault that the Phillips 66 was being turned upside down from all this attention. It was she who, in her sleep-deprived fugue state as a mother of two, had picked up and examined objects that Roz and Corey (and Molly herself too, before) would have thrown away without a second glance, assuming they were simply bits of trash the

35

wind had tossed into the Pit. Only in her post-Ben apocalyptic exhaustion did she find herself becoming entranced, staring deeply, dazedly, at the objects. Corey and Roz, and Shaina, finally had to take slightly more serious note of Molly's finds when it came to the potsherd and the Bible.

"It's okay," Corey said.

"If only we were still just a disappointing roadside attraction," she said.

There had always been a conversational generosity between her and Corey, an unspoken willingness to strive for wittiness, to laugh even if the wittiness fell flat. He was a brother to her after all these years working side by side, confronting baffling fossils month after month, joking about their bewilderment.

"Well at least Roz is over the moon about the ticket sales. Have you checked our social media feeds lately?"

Though of course he knew she hadn't; that was his department, and she had never taken the least interest.

"Where's Roz anyway?" she said.

"Made an early run to Quincy Herbarium."

"Fifi Flower?" Molly said. The term always made her smile—Roz had permitted Viv to nickname her latest big find.

"What else."

They were all obsessed with the fossil Roz uncovered a couple of months back—or had been,

36

until the more recent distractions. The specimen was a paleobotanist's dream: a well-preserved plant with all possible characters (flower, stamens, pollen, leaves, roots). The blossom had bilateral symmetry, like an orchid or iris. But this flower looked nothing like an orchid or iris. The plant didn't look like any known species on the planet. As was the case with an abnormally high percentage of the specimens they found at the Phillips 66, Fifi's location in the fossil record was proving impossible to determine, no matter how many herbaria visited or experts consulted.

So Molly and Corey and Roz kept going, kept pressing ever farther into the earth, hoping that someday it would all fall into place. Nonsense converting, wondrously, to sense. But though the Pit yielded plenty of fossils to their shovels and picks, eight years in they often had no greater comprehension than they'd had eight months in.

What would it be like, she sometimes wondered, to have a job that didn't, day in and day out, defy one's understanding?

"I think we need a new name," Corey said. "The Pit Stop?"

Molly couldn't tell whether he was being serious.

"My in-box is exploding," Roz said, and Molly, already jittery, jumped as her boss appeared out of nowhere. "Can we hire Viv as an intern? Have you seen the parking lot? We should raise ticket prices. There's no way Fifi is in the orchid family."

Not awaiting their responses, Roz vanished as abruptly as she had appeared.

"Okay, so," Corey said in the silence that followed Roz's departure. They were both long accustomed to Roz's manner: curt, yet somehow charismatic. Then, looking right at Molly, Corey said: "Kids getting the best of you?"

"What?" she said, suddenly self-conscious. Was it her eyes? Her skin? She tried hard to not look like a worn-out mother. To not look much like a mother at all, here at work. To dress androgynously and keep her exhaustion to herself.

"Relax!" Corey said. "Nothing. Just, I spied you last night from my car, running through the ShopMart parking lot. You were crying, weren't you? I would've stopped but I was already in the left-turn lane."

"I didn't go there last night."

"It's okay," he said. "Molly. I've been there. I wept openly at IKEA last weekend. The lighting section. Dazzling. David leave for Buenos Aires yet?"

"This morning. For a week plus. But seriously, it wasn't me."

"Okay. My bad."

He seemed unconvinced. She was annoyed, but she considered herself the kind of person who got over annoyance quickly.

"Straight to recycling?" she said, pointing at the mail.

"Oh, didn't Roz tell you? She thinks we should start filing all of it, now that we're getting more every day. Just in case. I've been labeling file folders. *Death Threats. Hell Threats. Threats to Our Families. Threats to Our Souls. Threats to Corey's One-Night Stands*."

It was the kind of black humor that had served the three of them well in the weeks since word about the Bible had gotten out, but she found herself unable to smile.

"You're doing the tour, right?" he said, glancing at his phone. "Friday's yours."

"Don't tell me it's eleven already."

"Four minutes till. Thirty-three folks at my last tally. I counted from the bathroom window. I'll be in my office if they turn out crazy, okay?"

9

She stood perfectly still, trapping Ben's body (squirmy, squirmy) against her chest. She stared at the lid of the coffee table, trying to pretend she had imagined it.

She tuned in to Viv's ongoing monologue: ". . . said, 'Daddy, do you know where *The Why Book* is?' and he said, 'Mommy knows,' so I said to you, 'Mommy, do you know where *The Why Book* is?' and you said, 'Ask Daddy,' remember? So then I asked B, and I know that B knows because I know that B hid it somewhere but he won't tell me but maybe when he's two and he can talk then I can ask him and then he can tell me where he hid *The Why Book* but now I'm kind of mad that he hid *The Why Book* when he's a baby and can't even tell me where he hid it. But I think Dorothy has *The Why Book* too so maybe we can go to her house and we can take her *Why Book* from her and then we can leave one thousand dollars under her pillow—"

"Vivian," she interrupted, keeping her eyes on the coffee table. "I need you to do something really important right this second."

"What?" Viv whispered, immediately quiet, alert.

"One, you need to get off the toilet all by yourself. Two, you need to go and open the hall closet. Three, you need to reach way into the back and find the bat. Four, you need to bring it back to me with your strong arms."

"What about wiping my vagina?"

"You don't have to do that this time."

"Yay, I'm so excited to not wipe my vagina."

"Do it now," she said. "Do those four things right now."

She could protect the mouth of the hallway while Viv went to get the weapon.

Maybe the mere mention of the bat had frightened the intruder.

Maybe she could bring the bat down again and again on the lid of the coffee table until the intruder was knocked out or dead and then she could call the police. Never have to see him at all, no thud of wood against skin, no face, no words.

10

She put the human milk in the fridge and pulled out the cow milk. She turned on the hot pot and tore open an Earl Grey packet and poured milk over the tea bag as she waited for the water to boil. It had occurred to her for the first time a couple weeks ago what a bizarre drink tea is, and now she had the thought whenever she made it: drench some dry leaves in hot water, pour the milk of a different species on top. A savage beverage, viewed in those terms, yet it was the civilizing force she needed before confronting the tour group.

She stepped out into the slight brightness of March. A variety of vehicles in the parking lot: a few gleaming rental cars, a dented minivan, a gaudily painted hippie van, a pair of motorcycles, a trio of bicycles. Corey had set out four rows of folding chairs beneath the awning that once shielded the gas pumps from the elements. It used to be just one row. Today, the thirty-plus members of the tour awaited her in the shade, sitting or standing, one young couple leaning against a defunct pump. Beyond them, the Phillips 66 sign, and beyond that, the Pit, and beyond that, the highway entrance ramp. From the highway, it looked like any old gas station next to an abandoned lot.

There were four children on the tour, which gladdened her; most adults were less likely to be aggressive in the presence of children. The kids (siblings, or five-minute friends?) chased one another around the Phillips 66 sign.

One by one the waiting people noticed her, the clipboard and the name tag, *MOLLY NYE, BS GEOLOGY, MS BOTANY,* and began to shush one another. This moment always moved her, no matter the size of the tour group: the human pact to grow quiet, to listen.

But now that word about the Bible had begun to spread, she disliked giving tours. She was nervous as she greeted this group. You never knew who you were going to get—religious crusaders or feminist crusaders, suspicious journalists or suspicious scholars, inquisitive stoners or inquisitive senior citizens.

It wasn't the more ragged members of the tours who frightened her; the wildest in appearance were frequently the mildest in behavior. She couldn't put it into words, the quality of those who made her uneasy; often they took the most innocuous form. Sometimes they would give her the creeps for no reason at all. Like that unremarkable woman a couple weeks back. Just a

43

plain bony thirtysomething in jeans and a baseball cap and a sweatshirt slouching around at the back of the group, but there was something uncanny about her, something that kept pulling Molly's gaze over as she went through the motions of giving the tour, so that she happened to notice how the woman pressed through the others to get closer to the glass case (Roz's idea, once ticket sales spiked) containing the Bible. And Molly noticed when she began to tremble (though she was by no means the first to react strongly upon encountering the Bible). Their eyes met, such sad weak bloodshot eyes, how irrational and small of her to dislike this innocent person, she was about to interrupt the tour to say something to her, *Are you all right, Can I help you, Would you like to take a seat?*

But before she got the chance to do the kind thing, she was distracted by a flicker on the other side of the floor-to-ceiling gas station windows: a child running toward the building from the parking lot. A child who turned out to be Viv, followed by Erika carrying Ben. Sometimes Erika surprised her by bringing the kids over at the end of the workday on Friday. Corey was already hurrying to open the door for Viv, whom he adored. It was one of those rare sweet relaxed moments of motherhood: this late-afternoon tableau of her children with adults who delighted in them, this easy mingling of work and home, this effervescent eagerness to finish up the tour and seize the children. Viv raced through the door, through the small crowd, toward Molly; Ben attempted to fling himself out of Erika's arms, reaching for his mother; the people on the tour laughed genially and parted to let them through; the woman moved aside only at the last second, seeming suddenly to notice the children, and half bowing to them, the slightest odd obsequious gesture, though perhaps Molly imagined it; then, Erika and Corey spirited the children away to the back offices. By the time Molly's attention returned to the tour, the woman had disappeared. In the parking lot, a black rental car backed up too quickly.

In the Q and A following the tour, in the saga of extracting the kids from Corey's attentions and getting them buckled into their car seats, the eerie sensation the woman had elicited in her was overshadowed by everything else. That was the same day Ben got a random bloody nose at the dinner table, a thin red thread that kept snaking out his nostril and down his lips, chin, neck, chest, no matter how many times she wiped it away.

11

She held tight to Ben, who struggled against her. Viv had reached the hall closet. Molly could hear the doors sliding open. She could hear Viv rustling around among the coats and hats and scarves and shoes and balls and toys.

She looked back to see if Viv was coming yet with the bat, but the hallway remained empty. Her head was still turned when Ben stiffened in her arms. She jerked back around. He was staring at the coffee table, gripping her shirt with his instinctual primate grasp.

There was no sign of the intruder, no audible breathing coming from the coffee table.

Yet the coffee table seemed to possess a different quality than before, a new sharpness to its lines, a sort of hyperrealness, almost a glow.

Nonsense.

12

Molly led the tour group the thirty yards over to the Pit. She thanked them for their interest in this unique paleontological site, as though she didn't know what had really drawn them to the Phillips 66. She told, as always, the story of how Dr. Roz Moto, completing her doctoral research at a nearby fossil quarry, suspected and then ascertained (after some clandestine nighttime visits) that the field adjacent to the abandoned gas station was indeed fossil-rich. After receiving a small inheritance from her favorite great-aunt, she managed to purchase the land, which had been for sale for years.

It wasn't long before Dr. Moto's quarry was yielding a significant quantity of fossils—fifty, seventy, even a hundred per day. Peculiarly, though, about 15 percent of the species that she and her team had found in the eight years since the quarry opened did not match anything in the known fossil record or in our modern flora, which had caused a great deal of controversy among experts, including accusations that the fossils were fakes. It was frequently enough a challenge for paleobotanists to situate fossils in the record, and new taxa were identified all the time, but the quantity of mystifying fossils made the Phillips 66 unique. Dr. Moto had always liberally invited and warmly welcomed any and all paleobotanists, national and international, to visit the site and try to help make sense of their finds—but even so, comprehension remained elusive.

Then Molly made her standard joke (originally stolen from Corey) related to the fact that, sorry everyone, there are no signs of dinosaurs at this paleo*botany* site. Think how many more leaves there are on the planet than animals; so, plant fossils are a lot more common than animal fossils, if not quite as exciting.

Molly led them back to the old gas station, which housed, in its front half, the ad hoc display room overcrowded with glass cases exhibiting the most impressive and enigmatic fossils ever excavated at the site; once Roz concluded there was nothing more they could understand about Fifi Flower at this time, it would be added to the mix. Roz's in-depth typed analysis of each fossil often went unread, especially nowadays. As soon as the tour group passed through the doorway, Molly could sense people peering across the room, straining toward the curio corner, the two small glass cases dedicated to the handful of human artifacts she had uncovered in the Pit over the course of the past nine months. She always waited until the very end of the tour to show them the Bible—less time for emotions to flare.

Increasingly she was coming to believe that she ought to have kept the objects in the cardboard box under her desk. Hidden, private. Why had she felt so strongly the urge to share them, especially the Bible?

Molly presented the various fossils, doing everything in her power to engage the tour group, to get them to contemplate the fact that this or that plant had gone so profoundly extinct that it was marooned without linkages in the fossil record.

But when the time finally came to approach the two glass cases of human artifacts, she fell silent. She allowed them to experience it for themselves, just as she had experienced it alone at the bottom of the Pit: the eeriness of a recognizable object that was slightly yet fundamentally off. A glass Coca-Cola bottle with the unmistakable white script tilting to the left rather than to the right on the red background. *Wait, am I imagining this?* A rusty Altoids tin that was a bit deeper and narrower than usual. The gorgeous hint of potsherd. And, Viv's favorite: the small plastic soldier with a monkey tail emerging through a hole in the back of his uniform.

"Is this a museum or a dream?" a girl in a wheelchair had asked on a tour a few days back.

Molly agreed with Shaina's (and Corey's, and

Roz's) assessment that a sophisticated prank was the most sensible explanation. Yet how could any prankster—no matter how skilled—achieve such authenticity, such perfection, with such a random array of items from different time periods? Aside from their eccentricities, the artifacts seemed to correspond to similar known objects from specific eras: the pre-Columbian potsherd, the Bible from the early 1900s, the toy soldier from the 1960s, the Coca-Cola bottle from the mid-1970s, the Altoids tin from the 1980s.

Anyhow: on the tours, Molly let the objects speak for themselves.

The Bible was small, five and a half inches by three and three-quarters inches, an inch and a half thick; slightly water-damaged on the lower right-hand corner; its maroon binding worn to pink in places; the words *HOLY BIBLE* golden on the cover.

It looked like any other old-fashioned Bible.

Roz had left it open in the glass case to the first page of text:

> *In the beginning God created the heaven and the earth.*
> *And the earth was without form, and void; and darkness was upon the face of the deep.*
> *And the Spirit of God moved upon the face of the waters.*

*And God said, Let there be light: and
there was light.
And God saw the light, that it was good:
and God divided the light from the
darkness.
And God called the light Day, and the
darkness she called Night.*

The tour group pressed in around the glass
case, while the children, bored, ran figure-eight
loops among the cases containing fossils. Several
people moved their mouths over the well-known
words; Molly took in their faces, their awe, and it
carried her once again toward her own awe.

Every time she saw the Bible, even there
beneath the glass, Molly experienced the same
dangerous charge, that buzz in her fingertips
a month ago when she first carved away the
dirt around it. The bliss of spotting that maroon
edge, the shock that she hadn't noticed it until
this second, the ridiculous passing conviction
that it had just sprung into existence. She felt the
slightest sensation of heightened gravity at that
moment; even now she could sometimes almost
feel it, an extra heaviness tugging at her in the Pit.

Before calling Shaina, she had picked up the
Bible, brushed it off.

To open it to this first page. To skim the familiar
language. To crash into the new pronoun.

The divine pronoun.

13

Her eyes were still fixed on the coffee table when she heard Viv coming down the hallway behind her, that combined resoluteness and lightness of her footsteps. While she was pregnant with Viv she had imagined having a baby, but she had never imagined having a child: a child who could be a sidekick, a helpmate, a collaborator; who could follow complicated instructions. Who could fetch a weapon.

She shifted Ben to her left arm and reached back for the bat with her right, desperate to make contact with it, not yet thinking of the thing she would have to do with it once she had it in hand.

Viv, misunderstanding, grabbed her mother's hand and gave it a squeeze. There was something so grown-up about the gesture, so fortifying, that Molly's eyes dampened, tenderness flaming up in her alongside the panic. The panic increased by the tenderness. She had to make sure nothing horrific happened to this child or her brother within the next sixty or thirty or five seconds. Her milk came down.

"The bat," she commanded in a whisper, pulling her hand out of Viv's, waggling her fingers with impatience, her eyes always on the lid of the coffee table.

"Okay," Viv whispered, placing something soft and leathery in Molly's palm.

It was the stuffed animal that Aunt Norma had given Viv last Halloween: a bat.

14

She was relieved that this particular tour group happened to include more smilers-and-nodders than usual. During the Q and A following the tour, back outside under the awning, they asked all the expected questions.

She was responding to the one about carbon dating (no, couldn't be used to date the fossils, since they were too old; no, couldn't be used to ascertain the authenticity of the artifacts, since they were too recent, with the exception of the potsherd, but since no organic material had been found in its vicinity, carbon dating wasn't an option) when it struck her that she was supposed to have watered her aunt Norma's plants days ago. She had intended to go over with the kids on Sunday night, but then David had gotten the call about the Argentina gig. Norma was particular about her plants, and her plants were particular too. Probably dead by now. Molly was wondering whether she'd have time to swing by Norma's after work (Norma's key was on her key chain, wasn't it?) as she called on the middle-aged man sitting in the first row of chairs with two of the kids on his lap, his hand raised high.

"Excuse me," he said, more loudly than necessary, "but you seem like a nice lady."

Molly immediately came to, alert. Anxious.

"I see that you're wearing a wedding ring," he continued.

She nodded reflexively, then clasped her hands behind her back, her fingers damp.

"Do you have any children?" he said.

She paused—Wasn't it a violation of their privacy for this random man to know about them? But what was the harm in his simply knowing that she was a mother?—before nodding.

"Good," he said. "That's good. That's great. Congratulations."

Was it only she who felt the almost unbearable tension, some threat muting the midday noise of highway and birds, something perhaps about to take place in this desolate field? Or were the people on the tour also staring at the man, uncertain, apprehensive, maybe even protective of her, their guide?

Twin droplets of milk emerged from her nipples, dampening her bra ever so slightly.

"Do you mind," the man said, "if my kids and I pray for your soul?"

15

Molly threw the bat on the floor.

"You hurt Batty," Viv said, stricken.

She grabbed Viv's hand and started pulling her down the hallway, back toward the closet, so she could get the baseball bat and guard the children at the same time.

Viv resisted her, bare feet planted on the wooden floorboards, her skin squeaking with each of her mother's yanks.

"You come with me right this second," Molly scream-whispered.

"But there's a deer in our coffee table," Viv said.

And there was.

The lid of the coffee table had been thrown back on its hinges. A deer head floated above it.

The deer head wasn't floating. It was just that its wearer was standing in a dim living room in a black turtleneck and black hoodie and black pants.

It took Molly a second to account for the sensation of simultaneous surreality and familiarity that overwhelmed her: it was her deer mask.

David's birthday gift to her. Her milk came down again, more insistently. He had made it of papiermâché and spray-painted it gold. The mask, which covered the entire head, had a slender snout, narrow eyes, sharp antlers.

She gripped her children as though the three of them were poised at the edge of a cliff, wind whipping around them, pebbles giving way beneath them. She could not move. She did not know how to pass through the next seconds of her life.

By some impossible sleight of hand, Viv slipped her fingers out of Molly's grasp.

The child's motion broke her mother's stillness.

Molly cried out twice, once at Viv and a second time for help.

But Viv was already stepping away from her, was already reaching to retrieve something from the deer's black-gloved hands: *The Why Book.*

16

The man who wanted to pray for her soul loaded his kids into the dented minivan and pulled out of the parking lot. She stood under the awning, watching, making sure they were gone.

Despite his question, the Q and A had ended placidly enough, a smattering of applause, a couple of shy stragglers—the only genuine paleobotany buffs on the tour—sticking around to ask her about particular fossils.

She wasn't proud of her response to his question—a nod, a smile, a murmured *Thank you,* and moving on. She was unimpressed with herself: unbrave, adverse to friction, her outrage mute.

But then again, what if his question hadn't been intended aggressively? What if he was actually trying to be kind?

She was impatient to tell Corey about the man who wanted to pray for her soul, but she didn't dare mention it to Roz, who was sitting at her desk in the former snack aisle, licking an envelope. Her elbows pointing sharply outward. Molly could already imagine Roz's flat, flinty reaction to her unease. *Yeah, so?*

"Licking envelopes," Roz said, "is very primal. Tour okay?"

"Fine," Molly said.

"Did you see this?" Roz extricated a magazine (hip font, muted colors) from the anarchy of her desk, the endless grant proposals and scientific publications and unpaid bills and whatever else, sending a cascade of paper to the floor but making no move to clean it up. " '. . . a bizarre new attraction for your next road trip, Americana to the max,' " she read. "Is that condescending?" Without waiting for Molly's reply, she flicked on the light of her compound microscope and began fiddling with the dials.

"I'm going to the Pit," Molly said.

"Don't work too hard." But Roz expected everyone around her to work too hard all the time.

Molly found Corey in the lab, using a dental pick to unveil a *Macginitiea* leaf. He hummed sympathetically but distractedly as she told him about the man on her tour. She stopped short of saying what she was really thinking: *Should we be more worried about all these threats? Should we stop giving tours?*

"Look, I'll take the four p.m. for you," he said, putting down the dental pick and plucking up a needle. She and Roz mocked him for his tendency to use random utensils to prep fossils; still, he was the best prepper among them.

"You sure?" she said. It had only halfway been her intention to get him to make this offer. There hadn't even been a 4:00 p.m. Friday tour until it had become a necessity three weeks before.

"Perfect way to start the weekend," he said, sarcastic yet sincere.

Before heading out to the Pit, Molly stopped by the display room. She loved it at this time of day, between tours, the lights off, the fossils and artifacts emitting a certain quality of silence, a certain fragrance of dust. She wasn't religious, but this Bible did something to her, quickened her blood. *And God called the dry land Earth; and the gathering together of the waters she called Seas: and God saw that it was good.* Without quite meaning to, she pressed her hands together, as though to pray.

The woman at the British and Foreign Bible Society had been aghast when Molly called to ask if their organization had, in the early 1900s, printed a version of the Bible in which the pronoun for God was female. "But I have one such copy in my hands right now," Molly was explaining as the woman hung up.

Usually she was pleased to descend into the Pit, a little break from the rest of her life, no one requesting milk from her body or asking her why pee is yellow. But today, as she made her way down, she missed the children vastly, painfully, to the point of distraction.

She missed David too: pictured him at the airport, going through security with multiple instruments, the large cases surely raising suspicions as they always did, schlepping them around during his layover, soon to board a plane that would take him so very far away.

Yet eventually the familiar process, the pattern of shovel, chisel, hammer, razor blade, soothed her, absorbed her, as it had for all these years. Her focus took hold of her and time passed around her. In the Pit, in times of observation, she forgot that she was a mother. That she existed at all, really, except as a pair of eyes and hands.

She worked too hard for a few hours, making up for the penny's interruption to the day's fieldwork. The earth offered up eight broken specimens, leaf varieties of which they already had many excellent intact examples.

When she looked up from her labor, the Pit was in shadow and the sky was changing color; soon she would race home to the children. She would come through the doorway and step into her alternate life, the secret animal life where she sliced apples and thawed peas and wiped little butts and let her body be drained again and again and refilled again and again. Where her moniker was cried out in excitement and need dozens of times a day. Where her bed was a nest with four different-size bodies rotating in and out of it, keeping it eternally warm. Where the messy, mobile chaos was the opposite of the hours spent in the Pit, engaged in the slow, endless process of carving through sediment in search of something.

17

The deer held *The Why Book* out to Viv like an offering.

Viv stopped midstep, hesitating, as though jerked backward by a magical thread, the thread of Molly's love, the umbilical cord tugging the child toward the mother, holding her back at the edge of the cliff. She glanced at Molly, her eyes wide and glistening, and Molly thought, *Yes, that's right, don't go, stay close.*

But just as she thought it, just as she breathed out with thankfulness for the fact that Viv, very nearly four, had the sense not to run toward a masked stranger, the thread snapped, and Viv sprinted forward to snatch the book out of the deer's hands.

Viv settled cross-legged on the floor and began flipping through it.

There was an intruder in the living room. They could be killed at any second. Yet her children did not appear frightened. This both distressed and reassured her. Was it true or false that children are like animals that can sense in advance when a tornado is coming?

Ben thrashed in her arms, wanting down. Her muscles were fatigued, but she forced herself to contain him. He grunted in frustration, straining toward the deer.

She felt the dizziness rising in her. She tried to catalog everything she could about the deer, tried to imagine herself filing a police report, detailing it all for David, but there was so little to note: the black clothing, the golden mask, his disarming stillness as he stood in the coffee table, the apparent confidence with which he inhabited their space.

The level of her vulnerability astounded her, destabilized her. David was miles away, thousands of miles away. And her phone might as well have been miles away, in her bag slumped by the front door; fetching it would require her to turn around, to leave Viv at the feet of the intruder.

She had only her body, her words, with which to save her children.

"Are you going to hurt us?" she was shocked to hear herself asking the deer, her voice quiet and even, an instinctual attempt to avoid alarming the children.

"Hurt who?" Viv said, looking up from *The Why Book*.

"Please, just tell me what you want," Molly pressed. She gathered herself and looked right at the deer. But David had made the eye slits of the mask so narrow that she could see nothing within, just the darkness of a face and the slight shimmer of eyes.

"What's this?" Viv said somewhere in the distance.

The intruder stepped out of the coffee table and edged back toward the screen door: a small, slim man. He seemed eager to leave, and she wondered if perhaps they had survived. But at the final moment, just before he exited, he raised his gloved hand and pointed at Viv, his finger sharp as a threat.

18

When she got in the car after work, the electronic beat for David's song-in-progress came on. He liked to record the background parts onto a CD so he could think about what to layer on top as he drove around. Before the kids were born, she would often drive him around in the evening, all the windows down, the volume way up, and he would stare straight ahead and listen and figure out his music. They would go sometimes forty-five minutes without exchanging a word, just driving in the dusk and the dark, but she always felt closer than close to him then, as though the car itself was his brain.

She still had the sense memory of his arm, weighty and appreciative over her shoulders as they walked back to their little house those nights after parking the car.

It made for boring listening, David's low looping rhythms with no melody, but today, missing him (missing him for himself, his wryness and his solidarity and whatever unpredictable thing he might say about the man who insisted on praying for her soul; missing his utility to her, to the home, another pair of hands to clean up, another pair of arms to hold a kid), she enjoyed it. The musicless music served to separate her from her workday, which had left her wrung out. It was a good soundtrack for driving past the stalled development, the exposed wooden sides of the unfinished houses and the upturned dirt hardening with time. And then the strip mall, the run-down boulevard.

It was tough, these unexpected gigs, being left alone with the kids for over a week with only a few days' advance notice. But they needed the money, always. Yet she was weary. She wasn't sure she had the stamina. She did have the stamina. So many meals, though, so many diapers, so many tantrums between now and next Saturday. The risk of someone throwing up; the risk of someone else crawling over and trying to touch the throw-up. What if the vertigo overcame her, those small intruding moments of disorientation? Plus Viv's birthday party tomorrow. They couldn't cancel the party just because he was gone; Viv had been counting the days for weeks. It exhausted Molly to picture the way the living room would look in less than twenty-four hours, the ocean-themed paraphernalia and paper cups and napkins and piñata detritus and cupcake crumbs and spilled juice. At least Erika would be there, inside the fish costume. Molly could pay her a little extra to help with the first round of cleanup.

"I'm kind of devastated to be missing the fish party," David had said to Molly in bed early that morning, whispering over Viv's slumbering body. Molly rolled her eyes at him, though she knew he meant it. He reached across and stroked Molly's neck.

It was well over a week since she and David had had sex, thanks to the whirl of their lives, and now it would be more than another week. So though she was too tired, though it felt like her breasts were currently the common property of the family (sucked by the baby in hunger; sucked by the child in jest, in imitation of the baby; sucked by the husband in desire; sucked, too, by the breast pump), she told David to carry Viv, intruder on their sleep, back to her own bed.

When he picked up Viv, she was so limp that her head lolled back and her hair dangled wildly, as though she were dead; Molly had to shut her eyes against the sight.

She kept her eyes closed until David came back in, locking the door behind him.

"By the way, Ben's not wearing his pajamas," he said, though his penis was already in her mouth.

"I know," she paused to say.

"Oh shit you had to go to him last night?"

She didn't have the energy to respond to the obvious.

"Do you think he's cold?"

"Can we talk about something else?" she said. "Or not talk."

She wanted to go through the doorway with him, into the other mode, where they were just two bodies with straightforward and ecstatic goals.

She was grateful they'd had so much sex together for all those years before they had children. Every time they had sex now implied all those other times, an accumulation of sex, the times they couldn't remember and the times they could.

How gentle, his hands on her head. They were passing through the doorway and she was glad. He released her head and she released him and she came up to him so they could kiss in the old way, with mouths open and accepting, the savagery of teeth, not those tame, raisin pecks of Mommy and Daddy.

It puzzled her that orgasm wasn't widely considered a phenomenon that challenges everything we believe about human existence—doesn't it serve as proof of an alternate state of being? Isn't the fact that people can feel this way, so in thrall to this enigmatic force, so carried by it, even for an instant, evidence that the state in which we spend most of our time is merely one possibility?

"I love you even though I hate you," she said to him after they had both come. She felt joyous, lazy with him. She felt rich, richer than a millionaire.

"I love you even though I hate you," he replied.

It was their shared motto for these early years of parenthood. Because sometimes you had to hate the person who was using the toilet or taking a shower or at work or sleeping or doing any other indulgent thing while you were caught in the cyclone of your children's needs.

About a week before, Viv had a restless night, coming into their room a bunch, so eventually Molly gave up and went to sleep beside her in her little bed. Then Viv slept well but passed her restlessness on to Molly. The next morning, a Saturday, David complained that he'd had bad dreams, a peculiar night of sleep, and asked Molly why she kept stroking his face all night long when she knew he hated that. "What the fuck are you talking about?" she roared under her breath so the kids couldn't hear. *I was tending to your offspring. Screw your peculiar night of sleep; I had no night of sleep. Believe me, if I had to stay up all night stroking a face, it wouldn't be yours. I love you even though I hate you.*

Now, beyond the locked bedroom door, a small voice was asking for them, but he had somehow fallen back to sleep in the past three seconds, so it was she who got out of bed.

19

"What's this?" Viv repeated, waving high above her head an envelope encrusted with golden star stickers.

"Where did you find that?" Molly said as she rushed (capable, now, of swift movement; of effortlessly bearing Ben with her, adrenaline whirring through her) across the room to lock the door through which the deer had just exited.

"In *The Why Book* of course," Viv said. She had recently gotten in the habit of ending her sentences with *of course*.

Molly darted over and yanked the letter out of Viv's hand, imagining new threats: yellowish powder, whitish powder.

"No," Viv protested. "It's mine and it's covered in my stickers and I found it and I get to open it of course."

"No."

"Give me my letter," Viv insisted.

"It could have poison in it," Molly snapped, her filter gone.

"What's poison?" Viv said.

"Something bad."

"Bad how?" Viv was scared.

"Just very, very bad." She put Ben down on the floor beside Viv. First she would open the letter. Then she would call 911. "Can you babysit Ben for a sec?"

Viv, frightened into compliance, turned back to *The Why Book*. "B," she whispered, "do you know why moths are not as decorated as butterflies?"

Molly went into the kitchen and put on rubber gloves and pulled the sharpest knife out of the knife block. She cut through the golden star stickers. A single sheet of paper fell out, unaccompanied by any suspicious powders. On one side, the paper bore an announcement from Viv's preschool reminding parents to please bring in extra tissues and paper towels (shit, she kept forgetting). On the other side, there was a numbered list, written painstakingly in capital letters in magenta ink. She recognized the color of the pen, which sat in a jar on her small desk in the bedroom. It chilled her to think of the intruder going from room to room, finding the pen, finding the school notice, finding the stickers, finding the deer mask, finding *The Why Book*.

1. GIVE V & B DINNER AND PUT THEM TO BED.
2. E BACK BY 7PM.

3. COME OUT TO CAR WHEN E ARRIVES.
4. IF YOU DO NOT COME YOU WILL REGRET IT FOREVER.
5. POLICE WILL THINK YOU ARE CRAZY.

So he knew their names. Item five notwithstanding, she would call 911, of course. But in her head her *of course* sounded as childish and misplaced as Viv's.

She ran to her bag and pulled out her phone, which had only 10 percent charge. There was a nonsensical text from Erika: *Yeah no prob c u @ 7.* Molly tapped in her passcode so she could read back over their texts. From Molly's phone, at 6:16 p.m.: *So sorry something came up is there any way you can come back and cover a couple more hours tonight?* And then, at 6:17 p.m., from Erika: *Sure thing, just postponed my drinks, actually works better anyway.* From Molly, at 6:18 p.m.: *Sweet thanks for swift response see you soon. Can you be here by 7? I'll get both kids to sleep so you can just chill.*

"No, Ben!" Viv cried out. "You're gonna rip it!"

Calling 911 no longer seemed like a possibility.

A text exchange of which she had written not a word, a text exchange that had taken place while she was crouched in front of the mirror in the dark in the other room—but how would she convince the police (POLICE WILL THINK

YOU ARE CRAZY) that she was not the author of these texts, which were indistinguishable in tone from every other text in her correspondence with Erika?

20

Her commute was short, the Phillips 66 less than two miles from home. She turned right just past the neon sign of the Excellent Laundromat. Even after more than eight years living here it still caused a physical response in her whenever she rolled off the weary, blaring thoroughfare onto these quiet blocks of tiny timeworn bungalows, the neighborhood soft gray at this darkening hour, an old woman limping beneath old trees, a dog mourning somewhere, a mild melancholy that resonated with her, the imperfect sidewalks and overgrown rhubarb and ill-tended crab-apple trees.

"Thanks for raking," David had said that morning, staring out at their small yard while downing coffee, his suitcase and instruments beside the door.

She had no idea what he meant; there had been no raking whatsoever in her life of late. But there wasn't time to probe, for Viv was pulling her toward the hall closet, distressed to the point of tears at not being able to locate her left rain boot. And Ben, who was eating his oatmeal in fistfuls with both hands, had just begun to experiment with tossing globs of it toward the ceiling.

Now, ending her commute, pulling up to the curb, pleased that no parallel park was demanded of her, she noticed how the base of the house no longer possessed its trademark ring of dead leaves. Someone or something (some wind?) had cleared away the debris of the dark months, making newly passable the dirt pathway around the house.

She forgot to wonder about it, though, when she opened the front door to a blueberry-stained Ben, to Viv parading through the living room chanting "Birth-Day! Birth-Day!" with an uncapped purple marker held aloft in her right hand like the Statue of Liberty's torch.

21

Her hands were shaky on the knife that spread the peanut butter, shaky on the bread beneath, shaky scooping applesauce, shaky slicing banana. Yet the children were tranquil and happy as they ate their makeshift dinner, laughing together at something that escaped her. She needed to be in a room, by herself, in silence, where she could think about what to do next, but there was no time for that.

As she shepherded them into their bedroom after dinner, she was alarmed at her obsequiousness. GIVE V & B DINNER AND PUT THEM TO BED. It seemed that she ought to disobey. That she should be crafting some plan, calling someone, getting help. Yet the instructions were sound, no matter what was to follow. Make sure the children are fed; make sure they get their rest. She locked the bedroom door and locked the window and pulled the curtains. She turned on the lamp.

This final half hour of the day, when she was toggling back and forth between the needs of two tired children, often felt insurmountable if David was gone. But tonight it felt sacred to hold the bin while the children cleaned up the blocks, Viv delighting in slamming each piece into the bin while announcing its color, Ben crawling over with a long blue one in his mouth.

"Red," Viv said. "Green. Green. Green. Blue. Red. Yellow. Blue. Blue. Red."

Would she ever again kneel here with them?

IF YOU DO NOT COME YOU WILL REGRET IT FOREVER.

Viv flitted and jabbed her fingers right above Ben's eyes to keep him entertained while Molly changed his diaper. Molly let Viv choose Ben's pajamas. Viv selected her old purple footed sleeper for him. There was an ice-cream cone stitched over the heart and Viv pretended to lick it. Her head banged his chin and he cried. Viv yelled at him to be quiet. Viv whispered at him to be quiet. Ben calmed down. Viv wanted to wear her whale costume to sleep. Molly talked her out of it. Viv deigned to put on her fish pajamas instead. Viv asked Molly to turn on the ocean sounds on the white-noise machine.

"Your hand is shivering," Viv observed.

Molly tried harder to still herself.

The three of them squeezed onto Viv's narrow bed so Molly could nurse Ben while Viv smelled his hair. Ben relieved Molly of the milk far more quickly and thoroughly than the pump, and she was appreciative. The milk had been accumulating for too long. Her bra was soaked. He nursed until her breasts were no longer hard and misshapen. She watched him float off into his milky sleep. When he was completely out, when even removing her nipple from between his lips couldn't reinvigorate his latch, she stood and carried him to the crib.

It was unnecessary, since he was already asleep, but she did it anyway: cupped his head, whispered a few words of a song into his ear. His head an exact handful, weighty and light at the same time. Holding him this way was as ecstatic a physical experience as dancing late into the night in a big crowd with David the way she used to love to do, their bodies and all the bodies around them nothing more than a manifestation of the beat.

She lowered him into the crib. A milk-saturated baby in a crib tends toward the position of Jesus on the cross, arms outflung.

When Molly got two books and rejoined Viv on the bed, her daughter seemed milk-saturated by association, slurry and sleepy.

"I want *The Why Book*," Viv stirred herself enough to declare. Molly could picture *The Why Book*, the bearer of the letter, on the floor near the table, surrounded by the crumbs and smears of dinner.

"No," she said simply. Viv, for once, did not challenge her.

Molly read the book about the rabbits and then the book about the mice. By the time she had finished the second, Viv's eyes were closed.

She stood up and turned off the lamp.

"You forgot my song," Viv accused.

"Sorry, I thought you were asleep," she said, returning to the bed. *You are my sunshine.* She was glad, weepily glad, that bedtime was not over. *My only sunshine.* That she did not yet have to think about what lay on the other side of the door. *You make me happy.* That she could continue to pretend nothing existed in the universe aside from this room. *When skies are gray.* This warm dim spaceship bearing her children toward their deep sleep. *You'll never know, dear.* She held Viv from behind. *How much I love you.* Breathing in strands of her dark messy hair. *Please don't take my sunshine away.*

Only as she lingered by the kids' door, petrified of what awaited her once she opened it, did she remember that she had forgotten to make Viv brush her teeth.

22

". . . a Friday-night beer with my girls," Erika was saying as Molly moistened a paper towel with which to wipe the blueberry goo off Ben's forehead. She paid Erika and then Erika was gone and it was just the mother and the child and the baby. She and the two fruits she had grown inside her. She was happy to be with them and exhausted to be with them. She wished the penny she'd unearthed in the Pit this morning had been an actual find and not a false alarm. She wished that man wouldn't pray for her soul. She wouldn't mind sitting quietly for five minutes and drinking something, tea or wine, before playing with the children.

But the children were already playing with her. Viv enlisted her in locating every pillow in the house so she could pile them beside her parents' bed and jump off. Ben crawled into the bedroom bearing a shoe and a crayon. He alternated between gnawing on one and gnawing on the other, looking expectantly at his mother to observe her respective reactions.

Sometimes when she was watching her children

she felt as though she were watching footage of wild animals in their natural habitat.

Sometimes when she was in the Pit she fantasized about understanding everything, even believed for minutes at a time that something crucial was about to be revealed, that the Pit was about to explain itself to her.

Sometimes when she unlocked the glass case and held the Bible it seemed almost to quiver with life, though she knew this was just an illusion created by the movement of her blood inside her hand.

The phrase *The life of the mind* passed through her head, followed immediately, instinctually, by *The life of the diaper.*

The life of the crushed Cheerio. The life of the soggy kiss. The life of the sticky floor.

It was then that she heard footsteps in the other room. She switched off the light, scooped up Ben, pulled Viv across the bedroom to hide in the far corner. She crouched in front of the mirror in the dark, clinging to them. The baby in her right arm, the child in her left.

— PART 2 —

1

On the other side of the door, in the living room, Erika was picking up the crayons. She had turned on all the lights and the room looked solid with light.

"I felt bad the kids and I left the floor such a mess, I'm happy I'm getting the chance to redeem myself," she said as Molly stepped out of the children's room and came down the hallway. Erika was the most energetic person Molly had ever known. "So what happened was we were going to meet at Tory's for the fries but did you hear their basement flooded? So instead we're going to meet at Beba, but later, but don't worry, I swear I'll rest up before my fish duties tomor— Oh, yay, Viv found *The Why Book*!"

How strange that Erika still existed, that she could stand right there where the deer had stood half an hour ago, talking as she always talked.

Molly experienced a deep unsteadiness. Everything seemed normal; she was disoriented by the normalcy.

COME OUT TO CAR WHEN E ARRIVES.

She realized that the whole time she had been putting the kids to bed, the promise of Erika's imminent arrival was in her mind like a life raft.

E BACK BY 7PM.

But now, watching her unflappable babysitter talk on in the friendly light, she was finding it impossible to locate the words necessary to explain what was happening, to tell Erika about the intruder, to get her support in reporting the incident to the police.

"Have fun!" Erika said as Molly picked up her bag and opened the front door and felt something take hold of her body, a magnetic force that pulled her out of her home and toward the street.

2

The deer was sitting in the dark in the driver's seat of their parked car.

They had two sets of car keys. One was in an airplane over another continent. The other she had dropped in her bag after locking the car when she got home from work.

Yet the deer was sitting in the dark in the driver's seat of their parked car.

She could have turned away. She could have run back inside.

IF YOU DO NOT COME YOU WILL REGRET IT FOREVER.

She pulled on the handle of the passenger door. It was locked. Instantly the deer found the button and unlocked the door and pushed it open and pointed at the passenger seat with a black-gloved hand.

Molly remained standing in the open door.

Her key chain, the unmistakable beaded loop Viv had made at preschool, the key chain that ought to be clunking around at the bottom of her bag right now, dangled from the ignition.

The deer had the upper hand. The deer knew things he had no way of knowing. The deer could destroy her and her children if he so desired. It seemed clear that a path had been prepared for her; she saw no choice but to walk down it.

The deer was perhaps annoyed, or maybe upset, by Molly's tears. He reached out toward her, both palms up, a gesture of exasperation or a gesture of invitation, surrender.

3

The deer was a nervous driver. Molly experienced his hesitations in her own body, the familiar anxiety of the left turn onto the thoroughfare. The deer head added to Molly's tension, and presumably to the deer's too, as it severely inhibited one's vision. She remembered how it felt to be inside that head, the smell of flour and glue, the shrunken view and the kids exclaiming and David asking if he'd made it the right size.

The metallic surface of the mask reflected the traffic lights, red and green and yellow blurs. The shadows of branches and telephone wires moved across the gleaming shell.

Was it possible that a concerned citizen, even a police officer, might catch sight of the deer, would be alarmed and act accordingly? But in truth the deer mask was beautiful; to any witness in a passing car, she and her kidnapper surely looked like a carefree couple driving around in costume, on a lark or en route to a party.

She considered requesting that he remove the deer head in the interest of their collective safety, but before she could brace herself to speak, the deer pulled up in front of the liquor store with the bulletproof plastic. He parked and got out and waited for her to join, which she did as in a nightmare.

The deer led her inside. There was no one in the store aside from a heavily bearded cashier flipping through a catalog behind the discolored plastic, blind to the scene of a deer escorting a woman to the ATM machine and wordlessly indicating that she should remove her wallet from her bag and insert her bank card.

Molly was quivering but she did not hesitate to do the deer's bidding. Two hundred dollars in exchange for her children, asleep, in that peaceful room, with Erika the dragon guarding the hallway. Perhaps this was it, this tiny robbery; perhaps after this she would be taken home and could begin the process of forgetting.

Yet when it came time to punch in the four digits of her passcode, she couldn't recall them. A series of numbers nearly as well-worn as her own birth date, but under these circumstances, the panic, they escaped her. Her fingers dithered, stupid, above the keypad.

The deer's gloved fingers shot under hers and entered a four-digit code; the machine rewarded the correct combination by ejecting ten $20 bills from its innards.

So the deer did know all her secrets. Molly felt cold, ill.

The cashier did not react as the deer paid for the bottle of Grüner Veltliner (her white of choice, though it was the deer who pulled it from the large refrigerator) with the money she had just handed over to her captor.

4

Back in the car, the deer reached to retrieve a gray sweatshirt from the car seat where Viv always shed layers of clothing and crumbs of food. He folded the sweatshirt and pressed it against Molly's eyes. It was a terrorizing thing, to have a kidnapper blindfold you, but she understood why he was doing it, or thought she did, so she tolerated it as he knotted and reknotted the arms. She breathed in the smell of Viv, that breezy dirty banana smell of child.

Once her eyes were covered, she heard him removing the deer head, just as she had predicted. The soft scrape of papier-mâché antlers against the roof of the car. And then the tug of gloves being pulled from fingers.

Her newfound blindness made it difficult for her to keep track of his choices, even in the known intersections of her own neighborhood. He made one turn, then two others, and already she was mixed up. She had transformed into an object being conveyed, matter in transit. She pictured the outskirts of town, one of those sparse desolate groves alongside the highway.

Her body felt bereft, untethered.

How tethered her body felt on weekend mornings when the four of them lay together in the big bed. Often Ben was naked, between diapers; often Viv was naked, angry if anyone tried to dress her. The mother and the father formed a circle around the two small naked bodies. No safety like this safety. The oxytocin churning through them. If the world must end, let it end now, when we are here, like this. Every single other thing—from the exhaustion of the week to evolution itself—is in the interest of this. This pure lack of desire. The need for absolutely nothing more than *this*.

She reached into her bag, desperate to handle her phone, her link to home. But what met her fingers was her key chain, the unmistakable beaded loop Viv had made at preschool, identical to the one currently dangling from the ignition.

5

She clung to the key chain in her bag as the kidnapper parked the car, as the kidnapper removed the matching key chain from the ignition, as the kidnapper walked around the car and opened her door and drew her out.

The keys the key.

The kidnapper led her up a paved walkway. She heard him fingering the key chain that had so recently been in the ignition. He unlocked a door. She tried to remember all the doors that could be unlocked with the keys on her key chain. Their front door. Their back door. Their car. David's basement studio. The Phillips 66. Her locker at work.

The kidnapper pressed her through the door and relocked it behind them. She recognized the smell of the room but couldn't place it.

She had the urge to yank off the blindfold yet also felt somehow safer in this artificial dark, letting her other senses be the courageous ones for a change. The smell of cinnamon, old fabric, Clorox, dried-out dirt.

Dried-out dirt. Of course. Aunt Norma's

kitchen. The deer knew all her secrets. Her botched plant-watering duties.

The kidnapper guided her to the table. She could see it in her mind's eye as she sat: the red-and-white-checkered seat cushions. The stove with the tarnished copper kettle. The window bars, remarkable in their ornateness (not long ago she had sat right here drinking tea with Norma, had thought how funny it was that something made to protect you from violence was also made so pretty). She had always loved Norma's kitchen, old-fashioned with its hutch and teacups, clichéd and cozy. It was no place for a kidnapping, no place for a murder.

The kidnapper took Norma's seat at the round table for two. He reached across the table and pulled the sweatshirt blindfold off her eyes.

She found herself face to face with herself.

6

She witnessed herself: the same uneven eyebrows and recently emerged wrinkles on the forehead. The same hexagon stud earrings she had been wearing every day for the past month. The dark cropped hair on the brink of needing another haircut. The angle of the nose; the placement of the mole on the neck. The color of the eyes, the capillaries showing in the whites of the eyes, the slight bags under the eyes.

She stared at her self and her self stared at her.

She was struck by their sole difference: the other woman bore a long, thin scab stretching from her right temple down to the chin. Instinctively Molly touched her own cheek, as you would if you noticed an inexplicable wound on your face in the mirror, but her skin was undisrupted.

The overhead light was too much to bear.

Molly looked down, trying to take refuge in the sight and solidity of her thighs, her knees, but they no longer quite felt like hers.

The woman stood and turned on the strawberry lamp on the hutch and turned off the overhead light and stepped to the stove and flicked on the burner beneath the kettle.

Molly realized then that the woman was wearing her old black jeans, the comfortable ones with twin holes at the crotch. She had searched for them last weekend, to no avail, pawing through every drawer in her dresser.

"My jeans," Molly said. The words sounded ridiculous, pitiful, in the silent room.

The woman studied her coolly from her spot beside the stove.

Molly focused on the fridge, the small magnetized whiteboard Aunt Norma used to write reminders to herself. It bore one word now, in blue ink, all capitals: *BLOOD*.

"I'll go by Moll," the woman said, her tone magnanimous.

Molly had always resisted that particular nickname.

"Moll," the woman repeated. "Moll. Maul. Mal."

Or maybe Molly just imagined the migration to the Spanish word for *evil*. But the woman's voice did grow more venomous with each repetition. Molly thought to fear the heating water, the boiling threat that could arc across the kitchen to burn her face.

"It's just because Norma has to have her blood drawn when she gets back from Arizona," Moll explained, her composure returned. "Earl Grey?"

Molly never drank caffeinated tea at this hour.

"Decaf," Moll clarified. Molly listened to the sound of her own voice emerging from the skull of another. "Not that you'll be going to sleep anytime soon."

Molly looked at the door. Moll watched Molly looking at the door.

"It sounds so civilized," Moll said, sitting back down in the chair across from her, "but what a savage drink. Pour hot water over dry leaves, add to it the milk intended for the young of another mammal."

She delivered this with a knowing smile; a visceral shiver shook Molly.

As she tried to resettle her body, Molly heard, in the far distance, Ben wailing in his sleep. But it was just an ambulance on the thoroughfare. Sirens (she realized only after becoming a mother) resemble the sound of a baby crying; surely no accident.

"Ben," Moll said.

It made Molly uneasy, the ease with which the woman said her son's name.

"You can read my mind?" Molly said.

"It's my mind."

"Where did you come from?"

At first it seemed that Moll was going to ignore the question. She sat with her hands clasped together on the tabletop. Her cuticles, Molly saw, were bloody, the nails ravaged by teeth.

Then, after a moment, Moll retrieved the twin key chain from the pocket of the jeans and placed it on the table between them.

"You know," Moll said.

"I know?"

"Yes."

"Where you came from?"

"The seam."

"The what?"

"The seam."

"The seam?"

"The Pit."

"The Pit is a seam." Molly intended it as a question, but it came out sounding like an assertion.

"Between possibilities," Moll continued. "Between different possible worlds."

"You came through the Pit?" Molly said, a dizzying dread rising in her.

Moll stood and ran to the stove, as though in response to the whistle, but the kettle had yet to reach full boil. She tapped the kettle, the hot part, with the palm of her right hand.

When the kettle screamed, Moll put tea bags in mugs and poured steaming water and poured milk. She carried both mugs over to the table. Only one of the mugs had milk in it. She placed the milky one in front of Molly and kept the black one for herself.

"You don't take milk in your tea?" Molly said.

"No."

"Then we aren't the same," she said. "I wouldn't drink this without milk."

"I used to be that way," Moll said.

"We aren't the same," Molly repeated.

"The Queen of the Elk," Moll said.

Molly hadn't mentioned her labor hallucination to anyone, not even to David; had left it behind in the haze of the hospital until this moment, when it rushed back over her—as her delivery of Viv approached, her inhabitation of the body of a great female elk bellowing on a grassy hilltop. She remembered the sublime pain, the big window at the hospital beyond which the sun kept setting. There was a storm or there had been a storm and there were black branches blown against a brightly glowing and darkly glowing sunset that went on and on and on and from the tip-top of her pain she demanded of David, *Why is the sun still setting?* and he said, *What?* But before she could repeat herself she had to hurry back to blow the great horn of the Queen of the Elk. Later, when she asked him what time it was, he said *6:23,* and then when she asked him again seven hours after that, he said *6:24,* and then when she asked him again three minutes after that, he said *midnight.*

Molly felt hot, overheated. How absurd it sounded now, *the Queen of the Elk,* yet how essential it had felt at the time, four years ago as of tomorrow.

"Six twenty-three and six twenty-four," Moll said, "seven hours apart. Tomorrow her—" She stopped.

"Your life is identical to mine?"

"It *was*." Her gaze was cold, condescending.

"You worked at the Pit? With Corey and Roz?"

"I did."

"You found a Coca-Cola bottle too? And the Bible—"

"Oh yes. I had my little collection, just like you."

"So—do you know where those things came from?"

"No more than you do. From a world where Hitler was just an artist? Or where Columbus's ship sank? Or where some cave woman ate one berry rather than another on one particular afternoon? Who knows."

A world where. A world where.

Understanding buzzed electric through Molly.

The thing she had known and not known for a long time. The unfathomable fossils. The unfathomable artifacts. Evidence of other iterations of the universe.

"What did Viv do in your world at three in the morning on the fourth day after Ben was born?" Molly had to ask. She still bore the sense memory of it: stitches straining while she crouched to scoop vomit off the bathroom floor while both children howled in David's arms. Later, when

David quipped, *Our cup vomiteth over,* she didn't smile.

"The floor of the bathroom," Moll said with a terse nod. "The strain of the stiches." There was something dark in her eyes, something dark and distant.

"That time," Molly said, frantic to test another secret memory, "nursing Ben when he was a month old and his palm happened to be in just the right position to catch a droplet of milk, did you—"

"Please!" Moll said. The ferocity of her voice startled Molly. Just one polite word, yet in her mouth it became a vicious insistence on silence.

Moll folded inward on herself, pulling up the hood of her black sweatshirt. Molly recognized it then as one of David's old hoodies, the smudge of gold spray paint at the elbow. Hooded, Moll stood up and walked over to the fridge. She opened the freezer and put her face into the coldness, inviting it to numb her features.

When Moll finally drew back, her face was shiny and incapable of forming any expression. The scab on her face seemed more distinct than before, a black slash.

Only then did Molly notice a companion to that scab, just above the clavicle, two inches long, hidden by the sweatshirt at most angles. And, nearly concealed beneath the chin of the chilled face: a pair of bruises.

Moll stepped from the fridge to the kitchen sink. She unzipped her sweatshirt and pulled up her T-shirt and unhooked her black nursing bra. Molly was wearing its twin, though Moll's looked more worn. She watched Moll cup the breast (same freckle), right hand on the bottom, left hand on the top, the exact position. Moll squeezed, and the milk shot out, six slender arcs into the steel sink. The soft hiss of milk hitting metal.

Molly stared.

"I've been hand-expressing for fourteen days," Moll said.

Watching it made Molly's breasts sore and her wrists ache. "Why?"

Moll looked at her with scorn. "Because I don't want my milk to go dry."

"You don't want your milk to go dry?" Molly couldn't come up with her own words.

"Do you remember," Moll said, "two Fridays ago, after the firestorm about the Bible began, a woman on the tour? A thirtysomething in a baseball cap and sweatshirt?"

A sudden hardness in Molly's stomach.

"The same day," Moll said, "I put up that photo of the kids as the wallpaper on my computer at work."

"With the backpacks?" Molly said, trying to ignore her ever-expanding terror.

"Even though that picture caught them in

between smiles, I thought it was cute, but when I saw it big on the screen—"

Molly's mug tipped over, milky tea spraying and gushing. Clearly her elbow had done the deed, though she hadn't been aware of it.

Neither of them moved to fetch paper towels.

Instead, Moll let go of her breast, though it was nowhere near drained, and rehooked the bra. She went to the fridge and pulled out the wine and got one of Norma's blue glass goblets from the cupboard and brought it to the table and placed it on top of the spilled tea and opened the wine and poured the wine.

Molly drank. Moll watched.

7

The wine was gone. Molly had drunk it too quickly. Moll refilled her glass.

"I'll come home with you," Moll said, "to nurse Ben."

It occurred to her that Moll wasn't drinking any wine.

It occurred to her that Moll had poisoned the wine.

It occurred to her that wine is already a kind of poison.

"No," Molly said.

"You shouldn't nurse him when you have alcohol in your bloodstream."

"It was only one glass."

"I can do it for you," Moll said. Her tone was casual, accommodating, but Molly was repulsed by the hunger shimmering in her eyes.

"No," Molly said.

"Let me," Moll said, reaching for Molly with her fingers, those bloody cuticles.

"Go nurse your own child."

Molly leaned away from her, just out of grasp, but Moll lunged across the table and caught

Molly's upper arm. There was something strange about Moll's touch, something searing even through the fabric of Molly's shirt. She could not bear it, the sensation of those fingers on her. The untended nails, sharp and dirty.

"My children are not here," Moll said.

"Back where you came from."

"They are not there."

"Let go of me."

"You have to let me. Because your children are perfectly intact."

" 'Perfectly intact'?"

"Your children are perfectly intact."

"And your children?"

"Your children are alive."

8

The brief relief (after pulling away from Moll, after being released by Moll) of the moments spent in Norma's powder room without that wounded mirror face, the sight of the face in the actual bathroom mirror, the straightforward act of pulling tissues out of the decorative hen cozy perched behind the toilet; for an instant Molly felt almost sane, moored by the Dove soap, the red hand towel.

But then, exiting the bathroom, returning to the kitchen, a cosmic precariousness. The anguish of the other was a contaminating force spreading throughout Norma's house, the hallway, the floor, the ceiling, and Molly found herself polluted, debilitated, by images she could no longer keep out of her head.

When he picked up Viv, she was so limp that her head lolled back and her hair dangled wildly.

Moll was sitting at the table as still as anyone could possibly sit. Her eyes closed. Not a twitch behind her eyelids. The spilled tea continued to drip and spread, untended.

The need to go home. The need to dispense

with this intruder, this nightmare, and return to two small impeccable bodies. The excruciating need.

Moll opened her eyes and saw Molly and made a gesture at her own body, her scabs, her bruises, the borrowed kitchen, the wine bought with money that didn't quite belong to her, as though to say: *It could have been you.*

They stared at each other, the Molly with the live children and the Molly with the dead children.

9

Molly was standing by the doorway and Moll was insisting on saying: ". . . and Erika died. And Corey. And two or three or four tourists. And, of course, that woman."

Molly was standing by the doorway and Moll was offering her water: "Here, come on, drink. Drink."

Molly refused the water. Instead, she said: "It's time to let your milk dry up."

Moll fell back against the wall as though slapped.

Molly ran out the door. She ran down the walkway, waiting for Moll to chase her. She fumbled too long in her bag for her keys, unlocked the car, leaped in, and backed up.

She drove fast. She kept checking the rearview mirror, picturing Moll behind her, racing into and out of the circles of light cast by the streetlamps.

10

The car smelled of stale graham crackers and papier-mâché. Molly took refuge in the smell. As she drove she thought: *something terrible happened to you but that thing didn't happen to me, I feel horribly sorry for you but the daily grind of my little life is mine and mine alone, why should I out of the blue have to share my children with a stranger, something terrible happened to you but that thing didn't happen to me, I feel horribly sorry for you but the daily grind of my little life is mine and mine alone, why should I out of the blue have to share my children with a stranger.*

Molly parked and jumped out of the car and ran toward her lit-up home.

She could see Erika in the kitchen, laughing into her phone.

But then, on the pavement leading up to the front door, a broken beer bottle, the pointed threat of the green shards.

But then the recognition that the shattered glass was just a few scattered leaves.

11

"—so my sister, you know, the one who's studying marine biology—so it seems like one of the male dolphins wants to have sex with her, and it's—like, she can't go into the water without—so it's creating some problems—it's essentially the same as when a guy at a bar—but she does kind of love this dolphin, I mean, he's really smart, but—"

"We'll have to tell Viv that a dolphin fell in love with your sister," Molly returned, her tone as bright and amused as Erika's, yet she felt like an actor—the right lines, the right gestures, the known world.

"Speaking of—I tried on the fish costume yesterday. It's kind of amazing, I have to say—where did you find it? I swear I won't say a word, she won't have any idea it's me." They had agreed that, in the interest of mystique, Erika was to be a mute fish. A mime fish. "I've been refining some pretty fancy fish tricks—Two forty-five, right?"

"Yeah, that's great . . . the party starts at three, so—thank you. So have the kids been—"

"They've been—"

Their voices overlapped, interrupted.

"—asleep," Erika continued. "No action whatsoever around here. Except my sister freaking out on the phone."

"That's really totally crazy," Molly said, as she was supposed to.

"Oh nice Orly and Jordan are here," Erika said, quick to notice an old Corolla pulling up in front of the house. "Amazing timing. It's seriously been one of those days when everything just works out."

"I don't have cash—can I pay you tomorrow?"

"No prob," said Erika, who, in a very slightly different life, had died two weeks ago. "I don't want to keep them waiting, they're trying to make it in time for the drink special."

Only then, pulling on her jean jacket, did Erika look at Molly's face.

"Oh," she said reflexively, as though taken aback.

"What?" Molly said.

"Oh"—she paused—"nothing, I'm sorry. I just had this weird—never mind. I'm a weirdo."

And then she was in the doorway, and then she was gone, she and her dolphin-sex stories and drink specials and fancy fish tricks.

Wait, Molly wanted to say. *Don't go. Don't leave me. Please, stay. Say "amazing" once more.*

12

Molly walked around her home, locking things. First she double-locked the front door. Then she double-locked the back door. Then she locked all the windows, including the one in the bathroom. She couldn't remember ever locking it before. She had to step into the tub to reach the lock.

Stepping out of the tub, she gasped, startled by the enormous dark insect on the bathroom floor, until she realized it was a snarl of black tangled thread.

She had to confirm that the window in the children's room was locked, even though she knew she had locked it. She opened the door slowly, frightened of them, of the possibility of rousing them, of how it would shake her to have to interact with them at this particular moment.

Entering their room was like trespassing in a greenhouse containing rare tomatoes, tomatoes grown from her own flesh. She listened to the tomatoes breathe. Her awe tinged with horror, disbelief, humidity.

This moist smell of their room at night: sweet and sour.

These two lives for which she was (irrevocably, unbearably) responsible.

Back in the living room, she pulled down all the blinds. She wanted her home to feel like a closed box, a self-contained unit capable of levitation, inaccessible and impenetrable.

But: that set of identical keys, somewhere nearby, moving through the night, weighing down a pocket or a hand.

She sat on the couch. She put her feet on the coffee table, stunned by the serenity of her home.

— PART 3 —

1

A baby was crying.

It was 5:03 in the morning.

A baby was crying and then a child was crying too.

She lay in bliss on the other side of the door, listening to them, their lungs and fervor. She wanted to listen to them forever.

But her delay caused the cries to escalate to such a pitch that, by 5:06, she was extricating herself from the makeshift bed she had thrown together in the hallway outside their room, was rushing exuberant through their doorway.

She rescued the baby from the crib and plopped him down on his sister's bed. They were both still crying but had lost their commitment to it now that its target had arrived. They began to distract each other. The baby pressed his face into his sister's neck. She squirmed at the flutter of his damp eyelashes against her skin.

"Pee-pee-peacock," the sister called the brother.

"Happy birthday," Molly said to Viv.

"Presents?" Viv said.

"Later. At your party."

The children wrestled on the bed, alternately laughing and squawking, and she watched them, obsessed with them, as though both had been born overnight. They were whole, perfect. She didn't recall any time when they had interfered with her sleep, drained her day with their demands. She saw how they filled her home outrageously, with a force far larger than they were, like angels or aliens. Their skin so fresh it was as though they had automatic halos around every part of them.

From 5:07 until 5:13, it was: Look at his hand, twining into her hair! Look at her fingers, unsnapping his pajamas! Look at his teeth, clamping down on the arm of the baby doll! Look at her calves, tensing as she stands on tiptoe to reach the breakable music box!

2

5:18 in the morning. A vulgar time to be awake. Ben was whimpering for milk and Viv was on the toilet, asking for some paper and a blue marker and a gold marker or if not gold then yellow so she could draw while she tried to push the poop out. And a book to rest the paper on. Please. So the marker would have a thing to press against.

When Molly stood up to fetch the stuff for Viv, who had historically struggled with constipation, Ben shrieked as though she was abandoning him on a street corner.

"I'll be back in a sec," she said.

She ran to get the supplies. Delivering them to Viv, she glanced at her toothbrush, fantasized about brushing the old wine breath away, restoring herself with peppermint, making some kind of plan, calling David. But by now Ben had worked himself up into such a state that she could hear him gagging on his own tears in the other room.

"Is he dying?" Viv said.

Back in the bedroom, she yanked up her T-shirt and settled onto Viv's bed with him, stroking his hot head. She reached again for the bliss, strained to see the halo.

There it was: the bliss, the halo, the guilt at her richness. The ecstasy of the ordinary. Two, alive. This freshly peeled piece of the universe nuzzling into her.

In the bathroom, Viv cried out.

Molly jerked up, picturing a key turning in the lock, kidnapper identical to mother.

"The blue marker fell into the water," Viv bellowed, "and I really need blue."

Beneath her Ben clawed for the breast with both hands.

"Mommy! Mommy!" Viv yelled. "Mommy, I'm yelling 'Mommy!,' Mommy!"

3

The children were eating breakfast. They were having yogurt and jam. They needed things. More yogurt. More jam. Spoon flipping onto floor. Mess! Wet washcloth. But this one reeks. So: another. Laundry, soon. Hands white with yogurt. A handprint here. A handprint there. Wait. Stop. Don't touch. Come here. Let me— Water, please. Wait, no, juice please. No juice. No juice? Hey I have a good idea! I'll make lemonade with that lemon! No. Too messy. I'll clean it up! Sorry. Not now. Too much. Too messy. Later. Maybe. Now! Cut it in half for me! I promise.

Under other circumstances, the same old thought might have crossed her mind: being a mother of two = ushering a pair of digestive tracts through each day.

But this morning she thought: *tracts, intact.*

She had an eye on the front door and an eye on the back door at all times.

The day was lightening. She was jumpy.

Something was going *tap, tap, tap.* What was going *tap, tap, tap?*

Viv was tapping the table leg with her spoon.

121

"Don't tap the table leg with your spoon."

"You're scary, Mommy." Viv was laughing. "I mean, you're scared, Mommy."

In the corner Ben made his sound of frustration, the *eh eh eh* of being a baby. He was clinging to the sideboard, reaching for the seahorse lamp, pointing at it, enraged, though she knew he knew how to pull the cord to turn it on; this recently acquired ability was one of his primary points of pride.

"He's mad at the lamp," Viv explained.

"Why?"

"Because it's only dark."

"What do you mean?"

"No light." Viv was not patient. "Only dark."

"Oh, the bulb burned out?"

"Of course."

"When?"

"Erika."

"I'll fix it, okay?" Molly told him.

He waved at her. It was his all-purpose gesture these days: it meant yes, no, hello, goodbye, bring it, take it away.

A farsighted earlier version of herself had stacked spare bulbs at the top of the hall closet. She returned to the living room with a light bulb. She unplugged the lamp and unscrewed the old bulb. The children watched as though they had never seen a light bulb changed before. Which, come to think of it, perhaps they hadn't. The tricky thing was removing the shade—it was impossible to achieve the proper angle of insertion otherwise. She stored each bulb under an armpit, not wanting him to grab them as she wrestled the shade. The shade popped out violently, springing her arms open. Both light bulbs hit the floor and shattered.

It was she who screamed. The children were silent, their eyes vast as they bore witness to the splinters of glass centimeters away from their bare feet.

She called herself names under her breath.

"Nobody move," she said, quoting what she remembered adults saying in such situations when she was a child.

She stepped toward the kitchen, circumnavigating the chaos on the floor.

"Nobody move!" Viv scolded her.

"Yeah, nobody," Molly said, "except for me," wishing it didn't have to be her.

She didn't need to repeat her command to them; as she went to fetch the broom and dustbin and a plastic bag, she kept glancing back to marvel at their stillness. They were children of ice, holding each other close: quiet, alert.

Only as she was sweeping up the glass did she remember that these energy-efficient light bulbs contained mercury. David had mentioned it to her, standing in the aisle of the grocery store. *Let's buy the regular kind until the kids are older.*

Mercury creeps me out. She had rolled her eyes at him. It was an old dynamic of theirs: whenever one demonstrated paranoia, the other responded with bravado.

"Kids," she said. "I need you to."

"To what?" Viv said. She always knew when her mother was rattled. "To *what?*"

"To leave this room. Go to the—your room. Okay. Take him. Do—blocks or something."

She couldn't see any mercury, no minuscule mirrors glinting up at her. Yet she would have preferred to see it, to know how much and where. Knowing nothing, she was left to sweep up the rest of the mess—at least, all of it visible to the naked eye. Then she got out the spray and the paper towels. All the while imagining small feet glittering with blood and mercury and invisible glass. All the while doubting that any of it was any match for mercury. But unwilling—too fearful—to search for mercury cleanup tips on the internet.

Was she done? She was done. There was nothing more to be done.

Perhaps she had not unleashed too much poison into her children and her home.

"Where"—Viv startled her, seizing her waist—"is he?"

4

He was not in the kitchen. He was not in the bathroom. He was not in the bedroom. He was not under the bed. He was not in the closet. He was not in the hall closet. He was not among the blankets and pillows of his mother's makeshift hallway bed. He was not in the other bedroom. He was not under the other bed. He was not in the other closet. He was not under the crib. He was not behind the door. He was not behind the other door.

"Maybe he's playing hide-and-seek," Viv ventured.

He was still not in the closet. He was still not in the other closet.

"We already checked there, Mommy."

He was not under the table. He was not behind the couch. He was not inside the coffee table. He was not in the cabinet under the sink. He was not in the laundry hamper.

"Mommy, he couldn't climb into there."

Was the back door locked? The back door was locked. But she could have relocked it. She was sneaky like that.

"Please, Mommy, don't make that face."
She had stolen him.
"Maybe he grew wings and flew away."
Wicked.
"Mommy, don't make that face!"

5

It was Viv who heard the single syllable: *Ba.*

He was in the bathtub, lying on his stomach.

"Ba," he said again when they pulled back the shower curtain and looked down at him. There were seven mismatched puzzle pieces in the bathtub with him.

"We thought you were dead," Viv said.

Molly scooped him up and crouched on the tiles, her back propped against the toilet, holding her children, but her children did not want to be held. They squirmed away from her.

"Sirens!" Viv observed. They were nearby, and coming closer.

"Sirens." Molly was giddy with relief. "That's the sound of humanity taking care of itself, did you know that?"

6

It felt like a small miracle to be here, in the normal light of the grocery store, the normal hum of it, the baby enduring his entrapment in the shopping cart with equanimity, the child gripping the lip of the display table, gazing up at pyramids of strawberries.

The strawberries were on sale; Molly stacked box after box in the cart, imagining a couple of generous bowls of strawberries adorning the table at her daughter's fourth birthday party, though the image of the strawberries was followed almost immediately by the image of their destruction, berries dismembered by imprecise baby teeth, smears of red on the walls and floors, scattered bits of green too small to pick up with adult fingers.

A woman with short dark hair turned the corner from the cereal aisle into the produce section.

Upon an additional instant of inspection: not Moll.

And yet.

Shaky with the ebbing alarm, Molly found herself missing David, missing him desperately, missing him as she had not missed him in a very long time, in years, perhaps. She needed him: the shape of his body, the balm of his irreverence.

But it was only Saturday morning; a week yet before he'd be back at her side. And she could not imagine anything—no wisecrack, no wisdom— he might offer that would neutralize the fact of Moll.

"You said juice," Viv was reminding her in the distance. "You said juice," Viv repeated, and her voice grew closer, louder. Ben was twisting against the safety belt of the grocery cart. Viv was pulling on her hand. "Hey, are there tiny cubes today?"

Brilliant, Molly thought; the cheese samples would absorb the kids while she finished the last bit of shopping for the party—the juice boxes, the rainbow sprinkles, the streamers, the other expenses and excesses of the exhausted mother. What a thing it was, grocery shopping, so tedious and so crucial.

She steered the cart toward the butcher section, Viv jogging alongside to keep up. It ashamed her how ardently she hoped the store was offering cheese samples today, and how glad she felt upon seeing the plastic pedestal, the ziggurat of cheese.

"Sword, please," Viv said. She liked the toothpicks even more than the cheese. But as soon as Viv had a toothpick, Ben wanted one too. He reached and strained.

"It's not safe for a baby," Molly said.

"Yeah, sorry, B," Viv said, relishing it, "it's not safe for a baby to eat cheese off a sword."

His face collapsed, his cheeks instantly covered in tears. It pained Molly how cute he looked when he cried.

"Viv," she said. "Don't gloat. That's not nice. I guess neither of you should get a toothpick."

"What's *gloat?*"

"Look," Molly said to Ben. "I can't give you a toothpick but what if instead"—she didn't know what was going to follow, something compromising, some devil's bargain—"I let you out of the cart?"

He stopped crying and smiled, knowing he had gotten the long end of the stick. She regretted her offer. But there was no going back.

She unbuckled him and lifted him out. Viv was on her third or maybe fourth piece of cheese.

"Viv, there are other people in the world, you can't—"

Ben was already at the pedestal, using it to support his unsteady stance, stretching for cheese and toothpicks.

"Wait, Ben, stop—" She swooped him up and grabbed a handful of cheese cubes and shoved one into his mouth.

"Hey," Viv said, "you got so many pieces for B, what about me?"

They could be dead. In another world, they were.

Molly grabbed a second handful of cheese from the display and distributed the cubes to the children.

"What's this no?" Viv said, chewing cheese.

"What?" Molly was trying to catch the dribbles of cheese from Ben's mouth before they hit the floor.

"What's this *NO?*" Viv was pointing at a sign on the glass case of the butchery. She had recently developed an obsession with *No* signs: No Smoking, No Pets, No Barbecuing. The Circle With The Line Through It.

Molly examined the sign. It depicted a woman with a shopping cart containing a baby. Beside the woman stood a child leaning against the glass of the butcher's case. All enclosed within a circle, all crossed out with a line.

"It looks like us," Viv observed.

She was right. It did.

"So, what's it saying?" Viv said. "No us?"

"I think," Molly said, gathering herself, trying to overcome the agitation the sign had set off in her, "it means Don't Let Your Kid Lean On the Glass." An explanation intended as much to comfort herself as to inform Viv. Of course they didn't want kids leaning on the glass, leaving their fingerprints. It was a generic informational sign.

"You mean like leaning on the glass like the way how I'm doing right now?"

"Exactly." Molly couldn't believe how chipper her voice sounded. "So don't."

"Okay," Viv said. "I won't. But I want to keep looking at this sign."

"But we have to finish the shopping," Molly said. "Remember, the juice boxes? You can have one as soon as we pay for it." She didn't respect herself, her never-ending tactics and bribery.

"I love this sign," Viv declared. "And it's my birthday. And I want to stay right here. Looking at it. Forever."

"We have to finish the shopping," Molly said.

Some moments later, Viv was on the floor, kicking and slapping the linoleum. Her barrettes had fallen out. She was screaming, not words but syllables.

Molly took a step back, clinging to Ben, who clung to her. Other shoppers had begun to assemble, to witness. Molly felt hot and helpless. The witnesses murmured and muttered, trying to help.

"I'm sorry," Molly kept saying to everyone, to the world as a whole. "I'm sorry."

She wished she had methods for ushering Viv back into her tamed self. But she had never developed any methods. The beast within fought its way out while the mother watched in awe.

As the tantrum continued alongside Molly's

repeated apologies, the witnesses either lost interest or trained their increasingly judgmental eyes on the mother.

The employee's name was CHARLEY, and she had a lollipop. She knelt down some feet away from Viv and held the lollipop out with caution, as one would offer a treat to a stray dog.

Viv—from her post flat on the floor—reached for the lollipop, the rope back to the grocery store, to civilization.

Molly was astonished. Charley tore off the wrapper. The witnesses dispersed.

"Charley," Molly said. "Thank you."

"Been there," Charley said. She looked too young to be a mother.

"Just let me say goodbye to the *No* sign," Viv said, queen of serenity. She licked her lollipop and stood too close to the glass case, petting the circle with the line through it. Ben wanted a toothpick, and Molly gave in, gave him one. He was pleased. He threw it on the floor.

Charley vanished. Molly tried to find her at the registers when they were checking out, but she didn't see her anywhere.

In the parking lot the cars glowed in the weak sun, emitting a color of light that seemed to come from another world. Molly felt slow, drugged by fear and fatigue, moving as though through water. She was thankful that their car was still there, right where she had parked it. But what did she think anyway, that Moll was going to steal their car and leave them stranded at the grocery store?

It was not the car that Moll wanted.

Molly couldn't go back home with the kids. Not yet. She wasn't ready. She needed to clear her head. She needed to figure out how to keep them safe. Her milk was going to come down; she could feel the buildup, that heaviness.

She needed to take them somewhere to nurse and play—somewhere Moll would never think of, so somewhere Molly had never before thought of.

7

There was one ragged forsythia bush in the median, issuing forth a few crumpled yellow blossoms. Viv greeted the bush as though it were a lavish garden. The ground was mud and old grass, but they found a spot where they could spread the blue tarp from the back of the car and it would lie mainly on the latter. It was a grayish day, yet weirdly warm. Molly took off her sweatshirt and used it to soften the tarp for Ben. She lifted her T-shirt and unhooked her nursing bra and placed her body alongside his. While he took the milk, Viv orbited the forsythia bush, whispering to it, pretending its smallest branches were flutes.

The median was in the nicest residential area in town, blocks of grand old homes. Though there were cars passing on both sides, their pace was sedate enough. She applauded herself for remembering about these tree-lined malls. On any other day, she would not have considered a median in a tony neighborhood an appropriate playground for her children. Who knew what the residents might think, peeking past the drapes at the exposed breast of the mother, the dirt-darkened knees of the kid?

But Viv was happy, encircling the forsythia with her magic spells, and Ben was happy, gazing up at the crisscross of branches as he nursed. The birds were out; they were nowhere to be seen but their songs were extravagant. It felt somehow safe, this muddy ornamental island protected by the threat of passing cars.

I can do this, Molly thought. She did not know exactly what she meant by *this.*

Viv wanted to play hide-and-seek. There was no place to hide on the median. The bushes were still leafless from the winter, and the three trees were saplings.

"There's tons of places to hide!" Viv insisted. "Just, come on, close your eyes and count to ten."

Molly squinted enough to convince Viv that her eyes were really closed, and counted to ten. *Ready or not, here I come.*

Viv was fully visible on the other side of the forsythia, but she had turned away, as though her own inability to see her mother rendered her invisible.

Molly left Ben in the middle of the tarp with his squeaky giraffe and made a show of looking for Viv behind each sapling and under each bush. When she finally stalked around the forsythia—those short red-panted legs bright among the branches—and mimed surprise, Viv shrieked with joy. Sometimes she seemed so old, filled with complex understandings, but she was still so little. Molly held Viv for the few seconds allotted her before Viv refused to be held.

"Hey why is B allowed to have that?"

He had crawled to the edge of the median and was systematically yanking bulbs—daffodils? tulips?—out of the damp soil.

Molly rushed over to him, yanked him up as he had yanked the bulbs. One still dangled from his hand. Viv was perturbed by the mess, the disturbed dirt and ripped roots.

"We, we," she fretted, "we have to fix it, Mommy." Viv crouched over the mud and began to dig. Her feet were on the median, her knees jutting out toward the street. "Hey a worm."

A car came by, too fast. The whoosh of it destabilized Viv, sent her tumbling backward onto the dead grass, and the driver, a thin woman, screamed something awful at Molly.

What the driver had said, though, was true. Molly felt crazy—crazy because only now did it strike her how dangerous this was, idiotic, their perch on the median.

She grabbed armful after armful of muddy tarp, balanced that on one side and Ben on the other, instructed Viv to keep close and hang on to Ben's foot as they stepped off the median, crossed the street, returned to the sidewalk, leaving the pile of ravaged bulbs and upturned worms in their wake.

Ben's diaper, she discovered, was leaking poop.

8

The kids were buckled into their car seats and she was sitting in the parked car, calling David. The car smelled of Ben, not the good smells of Ben but the bad smells of Ben. Viv, in the rearview mirror, made a big show of pinching her nose and gasping for air while the phone rang, went to voice mail.

Molly called him a second time, wondering why she hadn't thought to call him last night, why she hadn't called him this morning, why she had considered the median a reasonable place for the children. Doubting herself on multiple counts; unsteady with self-doubt.

On the fourth ring, he picked up. She could hear the sounds of rehearsal—instruments being tuned, strummed—in the background.

"Hey," she said.

"What's wrong?" he said, and she felt a flicker of relief, a flicker of calm, at how well he knew her—merely the tone of her voice, its slight unhingedness as she uttered a three-letter word, paired with her calling him twice in a row, and he understood that there was a problem.

Though now that she had the opening, his full attention from the southern hemisphere, she didn't quite know what to do with it.

"Something," she said, "happened last night."

"What— Are the kids okay?"

She didn't know what to say. "Yes," she said.

She could hear him waiting for her to elaborate. But what were the words, the words she should use, and what was the effect that they would have? Not only on David, not only summoning him back across the globe, frantic about her sanity, about the children, but also on her, and on Moll, making it all the more true by articulating it.

"Molly?" he said.

There is another version of me. She came through the Pit. Her children are dead. She wants our children.

"If you need to confess that you had a one-night stand with someone, can it wait till I get home?" he said.

"No," she said with a half laugh for his benefit. "Not that. It was—"

But then she sensed an alertness in the back seat, the acute presence of her children, and sure enough when she turned around there were four curious eyes on her, Viv's so sharp, so intent, her entire body perked up; Ben craning around the side of his rear-facing car seat.

"You're in the middle of rehearsal, aren't you?"

"Don't worry about it."

"The teapots are listening. I guess let's talk later."

"Well can I at least say happy birthday?"

She put the phone on speaker and held it up and David cried out, "Happy birthday, Viv!" and then a bunch of instruments started playing an elaborate rendition of "Happy Birthday," and Viv gulped and grinned, and when the song was over, Viv yelled back, "Happy birthday, Daddy!"

9

"Who is Ben's mommy?" Molly said.

"This lemon is Ben's mommy," Viv replied.

"Who is Ben's mommy?"

"This fork is Ben's mommy."

"Who is Ben's mommy?"

"The ceiling is Ben's mommy."

The kids found this game infinitely amusing. Every time they played it, Molly thought of a running joke she had with David, a question they would ask each other whenever the kids seemed eerily similar: Had Viv left messages scribbled in secret sibling graffiti on the walls of the uterus, information about what's funny and what's scary, memos that Ben had memorized in the womb?

"Again, Mommy."

For instance, that ludicrous stage they had each gone through at around nine months of age, when they screamed at the sight of yellow kitchen gloves.

"Mommy, again."

It frightened her how distant these memories seemed at this particular moment (the running joke, the yellow kitchen gloves), as though they were the quips and idiosyncrasies of another couple, another family.

She attempted to bring her focus to the task at hand: spooning their applesauce into two small bowls lined up on the kitchen counter. But her hands were uncooperative. Willing her fingers to still themselves, she carried the bowls to the table.

"Mommy. Again."

"Who is Ben's mommy?" Molly said.

"Ben's diaper is Ben's mommy!"

Molly shifted into autopilot, reciting her four assigned words every few seconds while Viv's responses sent the children ever deeper into hilarity.

She felt eyes on her. She kept looking out at the backyard, looking at the evergreen bush by the window, looking into it. No body among the branches. A relief.

Yet not.

The thing was: if it were her, had it been her, she knew she would be in the evergreen bush, watching, starving, envious, agonized.

It was where she would have been, wasn't it? So where was the other, if not there?

"Who is Ben's mommy?"

"Stop it," Viv was saying to her mother.

"Who is Ben's mommy?"

"I said stop," Viv said. "Stop saying that. We're done. We're done now."

10

Molly could always tell exactly when Ben fell asleep because his body took on a sort of god-weight, a sudden and exceptional heaviness that pressed her into the rocking chair, a reverberation of the god-weight she had first experienced during pregnancy, that superhuman bulk manifesting within her own body.

From the beginning she had felt that her primary responsibility to them was to their bodies. Enabling each to grow from two cells into trillions of cells, into a body, and then ensuring that the body kept growing and growing. Come on, go ahead, take the milk from me, take it that your body may become far bigger than it is today.

But now, in the drowsy bedroom, Ben's mouth separated from her nipple. His sleep lulled her to sleep. As she rocked him she kept losing herself for a few seconds. Each time she awoke she panicked, sensing an intruder in the home, forgetting and then remembering that Viv was in the hallway right outside the bedroom door, lining up fifty-two playing cards side by side. Viv loved the queen of clubs best.

"Viv?" she whispered, for the fourth or seventh or thirteenth time.

"Yessa?" Viv said, exasperated, her voice at the doorway.

"You still there?"

"Of course."

She needed to stand up, put him in the crib, talk Viv into napping before the party. But she was having trouble moving. If she could just stay here floating forever then everything would be so much easier. Her right foot had fallen asleep, as had a muscle on the left side of her torso. Sleeplessness was a drug, but so was sleep. A doorway to another world. She let herself go through, fine, fine, it was okay to go, the queen of clubs was babysitting Viv, there was this long gray hallway to walk down, a place that was not too hot and not too cold but just right, a place that was not too bright and not too dark but just right, and at the end of the hallway something was happening, something luminous, she hurried to see, she felt herself smiling, anticipating, but the luminous thing was an explosion, not a cocktail party.

She woke with a start, a jerk, looked down at Ben; he wasn't breathing, had her negligence in falling asleep caused him to stop breathing?—it had, it had!—but then, mercifully, he breathed, he was fine, he was not purple, he was the normal butterscotch color of himself.

She managed to rise from the rocking chair. With superfluous caution, she placed his body in the crib. She found a trail of playing cards leading down the hallway. She followed the trail out to the living room. The cards stopped at the couch, and there was Viv: asleep, hugging the queen of clubs to her chest.

The house had slipped into its alternate state of being, the sublime calm that envelops a space when its undomesticated residents are, at last, at rest. It was as though the house, too, slept, as though the walls themselves breathed, matching the pace of their breathing to the extra slow in and out of children sleeping, the lungs of the universe.

It was not right, she thought uneasily, not right at all; the ostentatious peace of her home, this deceitful normalcy, the rhombus of sunlight on the wooden floor.

11

She was slicing through the tape of the box of party decorations she had ordered online, extricating plastic fishes from among Styrofoam peanuts, when David called, the known ringtone.

Tears in her eyes at the sound of it.

Yet when she saw that he was requesting a video chat, she very nearly pressed the red *Decline* option, an instinct more than an intention.

She was scared of scaring him with her face.

He would see things there; he always did.

The reception, however, was terrible. His face pixelated and his voice monstrous. The room behind him looked dark and full of candles. His shadowy head moved glacially back and forth across the small screen. She placed the phone on the counter.

". . . it there?"

"One o'clock," she said.

". . . knew"—his voice, abruptly, clear—"two-hour time difference. So you—"

But then he was saying something else and she had no idea, the reception again fragile, his words a blurred roar.

It would be a relief to tell him. It would mitigate this dread. It would mean reassurance, assistance, a path out of the labyrinth.

Though perhaps he couldn't hear her any more than she could hear him. Perhaps her voice too was an indecipherable growl.

Perhaps it wouldn't be a relief; his incredulity, the weight of his confusion and concern. And his inability to alter any of the facts.

Then it was all there: the video, the sound, David in the room with her.

"—fast?" he was saying. "For the next seven seconds."

She noticed a bruise on her lower arm, a bruise whose presence she couldn't peg to any particular moment, surely just another tiny injury procured in the distracted rush of caring for the kids, yet it disconcerted her.

"—probably costing a thousand dollars a minute. Can I see them? Birthday kid?"

"Both napping."

"Lucky you."

She picked up the phone and flipped the screen and panned over Viv, asleep on the couch, still embracing the queen of clubs. He made a sound of love.

"Lucky kind of." It was easiest, she discovered, to fall into their regular patter. "If you consider sorting through a bunch of fish crap for party bags restful."

"So," he said, "what's going on?"

They had always prided themselves on their mutual brutal honesty: *Your breath stinks, You messed it up, You've got lint in your belly button.*

There's another version of me: Why not say it right now, swiftly, courageously?

But she could already tell it would feel wrong to say it, to bestow upon the situation the words that would give it shape. Her panic flared and her courage evaporated.

"It's getting fuzzy again," she lied.

"Can I see your face?" he said.

"What?" she feigned.

"Your face."

She zoomed the phone in front of her, giving him the briefest glimpse before putting it back on the counter. It wasn't candles behind him, it was three bare bulbs jutting out of an unfinished wall.

"Coy," he accused.

"Tired," she rejoined. "Fatigued. Circles under my eyes. You really want to see the evidence of how exhausting it is for you to be gone?"

"Seriously." His voice was curt with worry. "What happened?"

"Well," she said. "I broke two mercury light bulbs and she had a tantrum in the grocery store. What's it like there?" She couldn't even imagine it, some wondrous place on some other continent where he played music in the middle of the night.

"Lots of plazas and churches and the coffee's superstrong, okay? So tell me."

"I've got to wash a million strawberries before the party. I still have to fill and hang the piñata."

"You're breaking up," he said. "Piña colada for a four-year-old's birthday party?"

She was relieved to be breaking up.

"Okay, okay, okay, you win, Moll, fine, go," he said. "I can tell you're not in the mood."

Moll. He had called her that only a handful of times in the past twelve years.

Stunned, she held the phone up in front of her. His face was pixelated again. The little window for her face had gone dark.

12

She knew from *The Why Book* that Earth was rotating at a speed of one thousand miles per hour while simultaneously orbiting the sun at a speed of sixty-seven thousand miles per hour, and after he hung up she felt these two speeds in her body at once, and had to crouch down on the kitchen floor.

Perhaps those twin velocities, she hypothesized, explained the occasional dizziness that had haunted her ever since she became a mother, as though bearing children had somehow made her body excruciatingly attuned to Earth's double revolutions.

But it had never been this bad, a woman trapped on her kitchen floor, the tiles tilting beneath her, a kaleidoscope of trillions of Mollies, a Molly singing with perfect pitch, a Molly smoking a cigarette, a Molly tending a vegetable garden, a Molly in the middle of a car crash, a Molly failing to catch her baby as he falls off the bed, a Molly running shrieking into the ocean as her daughter gets pulled out by the undertow.

She forced herself to imagine a hand on her

shoulder, a still and solid presence, and the vision of that hand enabled her to at last open her eyes.

But it was not a vision. It was the hand of Viv. "Mother?" Viv said, which she never said.

13

It was Viv's job to remove the strawberries from the colander after Molly rinsed them in the sink. It was Viv's job to arrange them in a bowl. Viv wanted many bowls of strawberries, very many bowls, too many. She positioned three strawberries in one of the yellow bowls and stalked around the living room, speculating about the most ideal placement for this particular offering.

"We could fit them all in two big bowls," Molly said. "That's how people usually do this kind of thing."

"No," Viv said.

Molly was in no state to resist. She reached up into the cupboard and pulled down the entire stack of yellow bowls and placed it on the counter near Viv's stool.

Then Molly laid out the ocean-themed plates and cups and napkins on the table. She taped the streamers to the walls. The waste of it all, and the magic on Viv's face as the room transformed. The tape had gotten stuck to itself and Molly needed to peel more off, but her nails were too short, bitten.

The buzz of her phone in her back pocket launched a swift hysterical shiver through her body.

But it was just a text from Erika: *on front steps won't ring bell don't want kids to see me* ☺

Molly glanced at Viv, who was deeply absorbed in arranging yet another bowl of strawberries, and snuck off to open the door.

Erika held aloft an enormous bunch of silver balloons.

"Surprise," Erika whispered.

"You didn't need to get those!" Molly whispered back, moved to the point of tears: another adult around.

"Fish duty," Erika said, waving off her thanks and shoving the unwieldy balloons through the doorway. "But anyhow I had to rush to pick these up so I didn't have time to get in costume, it's in my car, so should I—"

"The basement," Molly said. "Those cellar doors in the backyard. They kind of stick, you'll have to tug hard. There's a bathroom down there too if you—"

"The square key, right?"

"Mommy!" Viv cried out in the background.

Erika winked and zipped her fingers across her mouth, my-lips-are-sealed, before closing the front door.

Viv gasped as she came around the corner. "Where's those from?"

"From a seagull," Molly said.

"A seagull!" Viv was in rapture. She seized the knotted ribbons of the balloons and pulled them, with some effort, down the hallway, toward the living room. "Look, we don't need flowers."

Molly was distracted, navigating the balloons along from behind.

"Because we have silver and red and yellow," Viv declared.

Molly and Viv and the balloons burst forth from the hallway into the living room, which was dotted with fifteen or so yellow bowls of red strawberries, placed here and there on every surface, including the floor.

"What if people step on them?" Molly said.

Though they looked, actually, very beautiful.

14

When the doorbell rang, Viv ran on tiptoe, the skin of her feet barely making contact with the floorboards. She was just now tall enough to unlock the door and turn the knob and pull it open.

The fish's scales were resplendent, iridescent. Its mask culminated in a fan-shaped headdress that descended from the crown of its head all the way down its spine. The tail took the form of blue spandex bell-bottomed pants. The fish wore silver sneakers, as planned, and blue satin gloves.

When Erika spread her hands wide to greet Viv, blue gauze fins became apparent, hanging from her arms like undermounted wings.

Molly had forgotten what a dramatic costume it was. Another item ordered online, scarcely glanced at before being passed along. She waved at Erika inside the glittering rubber mask, its metallic sheen and bulbous eyes. Erika offered a silent wave in response.

Viv was scared of the fish and in awe of the fish. When the fish extended a blue satin hand, Viv took it, majestically, and led her through the doorway.

15

Yes: the strawberries were dismembered by imprecise baby teeth, smears of red on the walls and floors, scattered bits of green too small to pick up with adult fingers. Also all the drawers in the kids' bedroom had been opened and emptied, every book removed from the bookshelves, the train tracks and the blocks and the cars and the dinosaur puzzle, a stew of toys simmering on the floor amid discarded candy wrappers, the enduring evidence of the mauled piñata.

In the living room the adults drank; the wizened parents of four-year-olds knew always to bring along a six-pack to these infernal birthday parties. Molly, sober, somber, couldn't bear the droll jollity of the other parents, they who rolled their eyes at themselves for having virulent opinions about various shows aimed at preschoolers, for considering a trip to sign one's will with one's spouse a date (as long as you spring for lattes en route). Three weeks ago, at a similar birthday party, with a similar crowd, she had been a force for droll jollity herself. Now she was fighting the urge to remind them that their children could die any day in any number of ways. Then perhaps they would not find it so amusing to gripe about the rotten pancake discovered at the bottom of the toy chest, about the inexplicable refusal to eat this or that vegetable that had heretofore been a reliable staple.

"Where's David?" everyone kept asking her, and she kept explaining. Aside from that she hardly spoke, four or five words here and there. The phrase *the tsunami of the party* was running through her head, and whenever she spoke, it was an effort to make sure those words didn't emerge from her mouth.

The children, caught up in their private momentum, grew bolder and more obnoxious by the minute. While the parents commiserated about parenthood, the children built and destroyed many towers. Molly gave herself over to the bustle of refilling bowls of chips, distributing juice boxes, snatching choking hazards away from Ben. She made herself dizzy from it, and when she took a second to look up at all the people idling around her overheated overcrowded home she could have sworn she was moving through a fever dream, a bright chaos to which she had no access whatsoever.

Dorothy's mother, with Dorothy's newborn sister strapped to her chest, asked Molly a question. It was a question about breastfeeding, about whether Viv had initially been jealous when

Molly nursed Ben. Dorothy's mother was a good-hearted woman who had incredible patience for in-depth conversations about sleeping schedules and teething troubles.

"Well," Molly began (of course Viv had been jealous, she was human, wasn't she?), "the thing, in my, in our, experience, about the postmortem period with the second kid is that—"

Dorothy's mother looked stricken. "You mean," she corrected, "post*partum.*"

"Yes," Molly said, "yes, postpartum."

If Erika hadn't been there, she would have been unable to endure it—but Erika *was* there, locating the bottle opener, catching the cup an instant before it tipped off the table, reaching under the couch to retrieve Ben's ball. And the children were enamored of the fish, their mad dashes through the rooms always lurching back around to her. They wanted to stroke her fins and scales. Molly didn't blame them.

A bunch of the children, Viv included, had crawled under the gray quilt of the big bed, pretending it was a cave. Erika yanked the quilt off them, exposing them to the light and triggering a spurt of screams, but their indignation was replaced almost immediately by delight, for the fish had a long blue rope, and it was clear that they were now supposed to take hold of this rope and follow the fish to the ends of the earth. Erika led them through the rooms, collecting more children as she went, until the blue rope was a twisting eel of small humans. The fish cleared the living room rug of adults with a few insistent arm gestures. Molly hurried to her phone to cue David's whale-sounds mix on the speakers. The human eel encircled the fish, and the performance began.

It was not much. Erika juggled three scarves. She gave each child a length of turquoise ribbon taped to a pencil. She had a bubble blower that produced twenty-plus bubbles with each breath. It was not much, yet the children were entranced, swirling around the room amid the bubbles, waving their turquoise ribbons, spinning to the sounds of the whales.

Soon after the fish show, the party fell apart. Viv lost interest in her peers and instead shadowed her mother, following her into the bathroom, where she intently watched her pee. As Molly pulled up her underwear and jeans, Viv said, "Phew, now I don't have to look at your skeleton anymore."

When they returned to the party, Viv wouldn't stop muttering, "IloveyouMommyIloveyouMommy," a mutter verging on a whine, leaving Molly equal parts touched and annoyed. Viv clung so hard to Molly's leg as she searched for the misplaced birthday candles that eventually she had to shake her off.

Viv wept as everyone sang "Happy Birthday"

(Erika bearing the platter of ocean-colored cupcakes she had baked yesterday with the kids), but refused to explain why. So absorbed was Molly in trying to ascertain the source of Viv's angst that she didn't notice Ben, straining to reach the lighter on the table, the beautiful green toy of it. It was Erika who scooped him up and away.

Molly lost track of Viv in the pandemonium of the cupcake distribution. She watched her own hands passing out cupcakes as though she were acting in a play in which a mother passes out cupcakes.

She was overseeing Ben's dismemberment of his cupcake when Viv reappeared at her elbow, bearing on her flat palm that selfsame hand cast in plaster, a gift from their kindly dentist.

"Please," Viv said, lifting the hand on her hand, "put this somewhere away from these noisy children."

Erika took the hand and placed it atop the bookshelf with utmost care.

The hand was precious indeed, a darling souvenir, a sweet little preservation of time, Viv at age three and a half, yet the sight of it always chilled Molly. It looked like an object associated with a dead child. David agreed; between themselves they referred to it as Viv's memento mori. Molly didn't like having it on display, but Viv insisted.

When the first guests to leave opened the front

door, a pair of the silver balloons somehow escaped the confines of the house. There was a light but adamant wind, and the balloons rose quickly, alarmingly so.

Viv knew, from *The Why Book*, what happens to balloons let loose in the sky. What they can do to sea creatures, and to birds.

"Call the 911!" she screamed. "Call the 911!"

The rest of the guests were escorted out to their cars by the mournful howls of the birthday girl. The fish held her as she cried.

16

Ben was asleep at the wrong time. He had crashed around 5:00 p.m., too late for a nap and too early for bed. Viv was sitting on the toilet watching *The Nutcracker* on the computer, as she had been for who knows how long. The exhausted aftermath of the party: Erika cleaning the kitchen (still in costume, to maintain the illusion for Viv), Molly bunching up wrapping paper and gathering snarls of ribbon and restoring the children's room to order.

Molly fell into the hypnotic monotony of sorting intermingled puzzle pieces belonging to three different puzzles. Under other circumstances, she would have marveled, as she so often did when cleaning up toys, that this was how she was forced to spend her heartbeats; that this drudgery was part of love, part of the mission of mothering a human. Today, though, she appreciated the concreteness of the task, the mindlessness, the scattered evidence of the children's vitality, the sound of Ben breathing in the crib.

On her way back out to the kitchen, she knelt

in the hallway, endeavoring to peel off the floor a sparkly dolphin sticker that some kid had stomped onto the wood.

She looked up from her task, at the fish conquering the kitchen ten feet away from her, and then she knew.

The fish was attacking the kitchen just as Molly would have: first the countertop across from the sink, next the countertop to the left of the sink, next the countertop to the right of the sink. The empty beer bottles in a row on the windowsill, rinsed for recycling. A few squirts of the orange-clove spray on the countertops, an unnecessary flourish but somehow fortifying before confronting the hill of dishes in the sink.

"You can take the mask off now, don't you think?" Molly said coldly.

The fish ignored the question.

Just then Viv emerged from the bathroom, and Molly was trapped: couldn't snatch off the mask, couldn't press Moll toward the door.

"I'm scared of the Sugar Plum Fairy," Viv said. "I need warm milk to not be scared."

Moll was already opening the fridge. She poured milk into a mug and zapped it in the microwave and stirred in vanilla extract and brought it to the table.

"Thanky, Fishy," Viv said. But, putting the mug back down after her first sip, she missed the edge of the table.

Viv and Molly and the fish stared at the white explosion on the wooden floor, a many-pointed star sharp with ceramic shards.

It was the fish who shepherded Viv away from the mess. It was the fish who fetched the dustbin and the paper towels and the orange-clove spray.

Molly sat on the couch, holding Viv, who was still shaking from the shock of breaking something so completely. They watched the fish clean up the mess. She was methodical, meticulous, and it was mesmerizing. They observed how carefully she scanned the floorboards for splinters of ceramic, plucking each one up in a square of paper towel, like a person picking rare flowers.

"Mommy, are you hating me?" Viv said.

"There's this phrase." Molly squeezed Viv close. *"Don't cry over spilled milk."*

"What's phrase?" Viv said. "Who cried?"

The fish perked up, looked up, as though she wanted to answer Viv's questions, all three of them, but then, remembering herself, she looked back down, returned her attention to the floor.

17

For the second night in a row, Molly went through Viv's bedtime routine dreading the thing that awaited her on the other side of the door. Once again, the dread cast the light of the sacred upon the mundane: the glow of the night-light rendered the toothbrush and the toothpaste and the pajamas and the blanket golden, as though everything Viv touched took on a mystical sheen. *Midas?* Molly had enough wits about her to remember the name, though she couldn't recall the moral.

She lay down in the small bed beside Viv and whispered into her ear: "We can't turn on the light to read books because it might wake B."

But Viv, as it turned out, had already followed her brother into sleep; the background whisper of his baby dreams, his body slumbering aggressively in the crib, had entranced Viv out of the known world.

Molly wanted to sway to sleep in the hammock of her children's breathing.

In her back pocket, her phone buzzed with a text. *So how'd it go, Queen Fish? Costume fit*

OK? Still trying to recover from yr bait & switch ;) seriously tho no hard feelings LOL, I get it. Give the birthday girl six million kisses from me. And then a series of Erika-esque emoticons: a mermaid, a dolphin, a pair of hearts, a red balloon, a kiss.

18

Moll had removed the fish mask and set it on the table beside her. Her hair was moist and her face looked rubbery, waterlogged. The sight of it made Molly feel as though she too had just spent several hours inside a barely ventilated fish mask.

She wished she had the baseball bat in her hand. But going to get it seemed more dangerous than standing still. Not that she knew what she would do with the weapon if she did have it.

Molly watched herself, her body yet not her body, breathing, blinking, shifting in the chair, adorned with iridescent scales. Moll had done something (picked off her scabs? put makeup on her bruises?) so now her resemblance to Molly was impeccable. Her hands folded on the table before her; her nails tidy, clean. Molly could not look away, the way sometimes you cannot pull yourself away from your face in the mirror. She sank into the chair across from Moll. She couldn't contain the twin sensations at war within her: one of utter familiarity, one of utter unfamiliarity.

"Share them with me," Moll said.

"I can give you money," Molly said. "I can give you my clothes. I can help you find a place to live."

"I can give David the letter when he gets back next Saturday."

"The letter?"

"Asking for a separation."

"What?"

"I had forgotten about it too. But then I remembered. Last June. That rage. Sitting at the kitchen table at two in the morning. Insomnia between Ben's night feedings."

"I wrote that in a nightmare. It doesn't even exist."

"But it does. I have it. You—I—we saved it in the filing cabinet."

The chair slunk out from under Molly. She slid to the floor. Pressed her back up against the wall. Covered her face with her hands. Considered the other secrets Moll possessed: the amount of stress she felt about how little money he made, the envy she occasionally felt toward unmarried, childless Roz, that night he thought she was happy when actually she was sad, the sexual positions that were more satisfying with her ex. The infinite blackmail material we all have on ourselves.

Eventually, the sound of a body standing and moving toward her and sitting next to her against the wall. A leg and hip and arm alongside her leg and hip and arm. A throbbing awareness, a sort of tingling heat, at each point where their bodies touched.

Molly scooted away. She did not want to be contaminated.

"You're evil," Molly said.

"Then you're evil," Moll said.

Moll's hand was too fast, a snake around Molly's wrist, tightening. She could tell that Moll was stronger, much stronger, than she had ever been. Two weeks leaner, two weeks fiercer, powered by grief. Moll's other hand now gripping Molly's hair, wrenching the roots. The tingling heat increasing to a boil.

I have suffered so much more than you, you woman of comfort and happiness, you unperturbed wife, you mother of two unbroken children, why do you keep forgetting that you would behave the exact same way if the tables were turned?

You aren't thinking straight. I'm sorry, but you're not well, you've been through too much. It's untenable. Absurd. To share the children. Think of them. How bizarre it would be to have two mothers rotating in and out. Even if they couldn't tell us apart, they would know—kids know—and they would be wounded.

The kids would be fine. It's you who would have to give something up, you of the perfect life.

When at last Moll released her, Molly's eye

landed on Viv's long purple marker mark on the wall. The mark somehow steadied her.

She went to the kitchen, looking back to make sure Moll wasn't following, and dampened a sponge and brought the sponge over to the marred wall. She rubbed at one end of the mark. The purple ink began to run.

Moll sprang up off the floor and lunged for the sponge and seized it.

Enraged, Molly reached to reclaim it.

Moll strained to keep the sponge away, her arms at full extension. She stood before Molly in this position of abandon, her skin and hair reeking of rubber, the blue fabric of her fins quivering. Her eyes urgent, unveiled.

"Don't wash them away," Moll said.

19

She woke up in the Pit. She was alone. The Pit was its normal color. So was the sky. She cried for joy, realizing it had all been a nightmare, though she was confused about how she had managed to fall asleep in the Pit. She was partway up the ladder when she glanced back and noticed a penny glinting down there, half-covered with dirt already, must have fallen out of her pocket; even though she had always been conscientious about avoiding that sort of contamination, she did not go back down to pick it up. She told herself she would get it first thing in the morning, but for now she was dying to get home to the kids. The parking lot was empty, which was strange, because she had driven to work that day. Or maybe she hadn't, maybe David had dropped her off. The morning felt long ago and fuzzy. She ran toward the Phillips 66, which was undamaged. She looked through the big window and saw that the Bible was there, its glass case not shattered. The whole place had its normal serene early-evening feel, Corey and Roz already gone home. Her bag wasn't beside her desk where she usually left it, which was also strange, but at least her keys were in her pocket. She wanted to see David, to tell him about this blip in her day and try to figure out what had happened. She would walk home. She felt elated. She would surprise the kids and David.

She would be happier than she had ever been.

She was wearing dark clothing and it wasn't until she reached the second telephone pole on the frontage road (a passing trucker honked and flashed his lights and yelled out the window, "You okay?") that she admitted to herself that her jeans and black shirt were hardened with a sticky, rusty substance. She had been so brilliantly ignoring the brownish smears on her hands, the throb of her temples. She ran back to the Phillips 66. She unlocked her locker and grabbed her change of clothes and went into the bathroom and washed herself and swapped the clothes and shoved the messed-up clothes in the locker and worked hard to forget about them.

She walked along the frontage road as night fell. She watched handfuls of birds reel in the sky. Her elation had dulled but she pretended it hadn't. She needed to be home and she began to run and by the time she reached the thoroughfare she was nearly sprinting. She treated the neon sign of Excellent Laundromat like a finish line. After passing the Laundromat, she turned right. She was ecstatic because even from two blocks away she could see that they were playing out in front of the house. She could hear them and she could see their bodies, perfectly intact. David was holding Ben and counting nine, eight, seven, six, five, four, three, two, one, ready or not, here I come! Viv was hiding in a silly place, in plain sight, only a quarter-hidden by the crab-apple tree.

"Got you, got you," David growled.

Got you! she was about to growl too when someone opened the front door and released out onto the lawn that Scotch-colored light cast by her favorite lamp. Erika, dear Erika, she assumed, but the children turned their faces toward the light and cried out, "Mamamamamama!"

"Spaghetti," the woman promised with her same voice.

By the time she reached the front steps, they were all inside. She walked around to the back. She didn't try to hide herself. She didn't sneak through the bushes. She had no reason to. The other woman was, obviously, an imposter. But inside, on the other side of the window, they were all behaving as though everything was normal, David carrying forks to the table, Ben reaching for the saltshaker, Viv testing each chair to see which one suited her tonight, David pulling the saltshaker away from Ben before he dropped it on the floor.

The woman inside passed by the window,

which she herself had pulled up twelve hours earlier to let in fresh air. She witnessed an instant of weariness pass over the woman's features as she glanced out at the dusk. How dare she look so weary. If the woman inside spotted the woman outside, she could have easily assumed it was her reflection.

"I got you something special," she heard the woman say to her daughter.

She had grabbed, at the convenience store on the way to work that morning, at the last second, as the guy was ringing her up, a fruit leather for Viv. She had been short with the kids when she was leaving because they had taken every single pot and pan and lid out of the cabinet while she was in the shower and scattered them all across the floor. "It's just pots and pans," David had said, and she had hissed, "Easy for you to say," and the children had stared at the parents with those four huge eyes of theirs.

The woman told Viv that she could have the special treat after dinner if she ate four spinach leaves and twenty-one peas; Viv had recently begun to find numerical precision very convincing.

She walked around the corner of the house, crunching through dead leaves, pressing forth into the evergreen bush in order to access the other window, the one with a better angle on the dining area. There was a sudden hubbub at the dinner table; at first she assumed their acknowledgment of her presence was the source of the crisis, but then she saw that Ben had a bloody nose, a red thread snaking from his nostril all the way down his bare chest to his diaper (someone, presumably the woman, had taken his shirt off so it wouldn't get messy at dinner). Viv was crying because of the blood. Ben was laughing because Viv was crying. David was running for tissues. The woman looked tired, worried and tired.

It was then that she noticed, there inside on the coffee table, her keys, the ones she had used not an hour earlier to open her locker at work, that unmistakable beaded loop Viv had made at preschool. How had this woman possibly gotten ahold of her key chain? Enraged, she reached into her pocket. But her keys were there. The exact same keys. The identical one-of-a-kind beaded loop. It was horrifying to see them both at once, Viv's random beadwork impeccably replicated, the implication of her still-babyish fingers struggling to string the beads, the image of twin Vivs laboring over the green bead, the yellow bead, the purple bead.

She left the window that was not her window and the house that was not her house and the husband who was not her husband and the children who were not her children. She walked all night, numb to the world around her. She walked in areas she had only ever driven by and areas she didn't know existed. At some point she slept on concrete and awoke beneath a highway overpass. She had no idea where she was but she walked until she recognized something and, after many hours, she returned to the house, to the evergreen bush. Her children were in the living room, perfectly intact, with Erika, perfectly intact. They were surrounded by hundreds of crayons and puzzle pieces and then they opened the back door and yelled at the squirrel trying to get into the bird feeder and it became a game for them to open the door and yell "Go away!" even long after the squirrel had gone away. She watched them from deep inside the evergreen until the mother and father returned. It had given her solace to watch the children but it wounded her to watch the family. Again she walked all night and slept somewhere. She used the toilet at convenience stores or squatted in the woods in the park, and she squeezed her milk out into unclean sinks or into the dirt, and when she couldn't bear her thirst she drank from water fountains, but she did not eat anything and she was ready to die. She stank and being a vagrant made sense to her. She didn't believe that her body was still alive now that their bodies weren't alive. She thought of the way their room smelled in the middle of the night, sweet and sour. She walked in the dark and thought about her errors. She should have destroyed the Bible, and the other artifacts too, without ever showing them to anyone. She should have been more scared of the threats. She should have refused to give any tours. She should have kept her children safe in a beautiful locked attic somewhere. A sky painted on the ceiling. She walked along the highway softly screaming and eager to die.

After a few days, though, when her head was clear from the starvation, she got the idea. She pulled the keys out of her pocket because they were all she had, and the round key kindly reminded her that it could open the door of Norma's house, and she went there and she cleaned herself and she ate mandarin oranges from a can and black beans from a can and she drank tea and she chose not to water Norma's plants and she thought about the idea. She slept in a bed and she woke up and she pictured herself doing it, step by step by step by step by step. She became deliberate in her movements. She considered different ways of going about it. She remembered the deer head David had made for her. She did not think about him, about his devastation, back wherever he was. She went into the house when everyone was out and she took the things she needed. She spied and she eavesdropped. She saw the baby slide *The Why Book* under the couch. When he cried in the night she unlocked the back door and went to him. He was thirsty and sweaty so she nursed him and took off his pajamas and watched him fall back to sleep. When the mother went to sleep with the daughter in her little bed, she went to sleep in the big bed with the husband; not sex, just beside him in the bed, smelling his neck, stroking his face.

She was crouching in the evergreen on Sunday when the Buenos Aires call came through. She watched his face rise and fall and rise and fall as the conversation moved from enthusiasm to logistics. She envisioned exactly what she would have done if she had been home alone with the children when an intruder entered. She anticipated the woman's every emotion, every action and reaction.

20

In the bedroom, Ben began to cry.

First just a whimper, and then the favorite syllable.

They both tensed. They knew how little time they had between his first sounds and his sister's cranky awakening.

mamamamamamama

It was no surprise that he was stirring, hungry, thirsty, after his non-bedtime. They both had been half expecting it at every instant. They hovered together in the seconds passing too swiftly as the sound intensified, the escalating need, the milk heavy in them.

Molly remembered, kind of, snapping at the kids about the pots and pans a couple weeks back. Remembered purchasing a fruit leather for Viv. Blurs in the great blur.

"My turn," Moll said.

Molly felt it like a solid thing, the awareness of her outrageous abundance in comparison to this woman, this refugee from a far crueler reality.

mamamamamamama

Molly was so tired, too tired. What she was

thinking about was the night a few months earlier, when Viv had first asked about death. *Can you please show me a picture of a dead person? Can you please draw me a picture of a dead person?*

mamamamamamama

Molly's nod was barely perceptible, a tiny giving up, yet that slight motion catapulted Moll out of her chair and down the hall toward the children's room.

The siren song of her baby screaming was unbearable to Molly, she needed to be tied to a mast, beeswax thrust into her ears, so as not to rush down the hall behind Moll and shove her out of the way.

But then the crying ceased, replaced by the measured glide of the rocking chair, the damp animal noise.

A sound, Molly discovered, far more intolerable than the screaming.

She would prefer not to eavesdrop on these sounds of intimacy.

She sat and listened.

21

Apparently it's an instinct, a holdover from the time when the infants of our primate ancestors would fling their arms backward in an attempt to grab branches and save themselves upon tumbling off the tree. It always looked religious to her, though, a gesture of religious abandon, giving oneself over to sleep as to a cross as to a god. Every time it moved her, this final divine flinch of his as she placed him in the crib after nursing him.

Moll was luminous, almost unrecognizable, when she returned from the bedroom.

22

She had never been able to decide whether it was a pleasing sensation or a disconcerting one, when you're holding their hands and you can feel their hearts beating in their hands.

That awareness of their arteries.

She remembered almost nothing. She remembered change scattering out of her pocket as she slid to the bottom of the Pit, laden. She remembered a penny in the mud. Her daughter is—was—always on the lookout for pennies, heads up for good luck.

It was hot, way too hot, at the bottom of the Pit. It took her a second to understand that the source of the heat was blood.

She was running so fast to get them away and then she ran over the edge of the Pit and they sort of fell down into it, the three of them, his body in her right arm and her body in her left arm, slipping and scooting down the mud, and because they were not laughing, she knew they were dead.

23

Molly was standing in front of the open freezer, drinking pomegranate vodka straight from the bottle. She had no idea why there was pomegranate vodka in her freezer. There never before had been.

Moll—aglow, atremble—came toward her, and for a millisecond, Molly thought the other woman was going to kiss her. But instead Moll stood beside her in the chill and light pouring out of the freezer.

"Alien greenhouse," Moll said.

Molly knew what she meant: their room, the rich outlandish smell of it at night, that place where small and perfect bodies were grown, the dark and glowing tomatoes.

Moll took the vodka from Molly's hand, screwed the cap back on, returned it to the freezer, shut the freezer. She shepherded Molly over to the couch, her hand too hot on the small of Molly's back, yet Molly acquiesced like a child. The world was spiraling, unreliable, her arms disobedient, her legs monstrous in their defiance of her intentions.

The weight of two small corpses.

Moll went back to the kitchen and turned on the faucet and rinsed an apple.

When Molly was upset, it calmed her to drink water and eat an apple.

She watched Moll move around her kitchen, linger over the wooden knife block, fish scales shimmering.

Moll looked at Molly and pulled out the largest knife—a preposterous knife to use on an apple. She held it up, almost brandished it. Seeing the knife gleam in the kitchen light, Molly knew what she would do if she were Moll. Knew she would do it at knifepoint, at gunpoint, as necessary. But then the knife descended on the apple, and Moll was merely a woman cutting an apple.

Moll strode over to the couch, bearing a plate of sliced apple in one hand and a big mason jar filled with water in the other.

It was her favorite thing to drink out of, a big mason jar.

But she did not dare to eat this apple. She did not dare to drink this water.

24

She couldn't put it into words, the quality of those who made her uneasy; often they took the most innocuous form. Sometimes they would give her the creeps for no reason at all.

Something kept pulling her gaze over to the unremarkable woman (plain, bony, thirtysomething, jeans and baseball cap and sweatshirt) as she went through the motions of giving the tour, so that she happened to notice how the woman pressed through the others to get closer to the glass case containing the Bible. And she noticed when the woman began to tremble (though she was by no means the first to react strongly upon encountering the Bible).

Their eyes met, such sad weak bloodshot eyes, how irrational and small of her to dislike this innocent person; the woman was shaking harder by the second and she saw that she needed help. She imagined that this was one of her own children thirty years from now, suffering through a difficult day, quaking with private grief. She would do the kind thing. She took a step toward the woman.

"Are you all right?" she said, interrupting the tour. "Can I help you?"

As she spoke, she noticed a flicker on the other side of the floor-to-ceiling gas station windows: a child running toward the building from the parking lot. A child who turned out to be Viv, followed by Erika carrying Ben. Corey had already spotted them, was hurrying to open the door for Viv.

She had just been thinking of her children and now here they were, as though her thought had given them body. She was pleased—self-congratulatory—that they had arrived when she was engaged in an act of compassion.

"Would you like to take a seat?" she said to the woman.

Behind the quaking woman, not visible to the quaking woman, Viv was racing through the door, through the small crowd; Ben was attempting to fling himself out of Erika's arms, reaching in the direction of his mother.

The woman was staring at her, fearful, fragile. She reached to catch the woman in case she fell. But the woman backed away from her, edging closer to the glass case containing the Bible, closer to the doorway where the children just entered.

The woman reached one hand high up into the air and placed one hand against her stomach. She was crying. Then she reached under her sweatshirt, pressed herself somewhere, and detonated.

— PART 4 —

1

The metallic scrape of the slanted cellar doors (they had never quite joined properly), steel on brick, that familiar painful yank, the sound aching in her teeth.

It was early yet; she assumed she would be waking her. But coming down the steep stairs she saw that she was already awake, perhaps long awake, sitting cross-legged on the worn-out rug in the flat morning light, eerily alert. None of the lamps were on; so she had been waiting in the dark. The futon was in its couch form. The sheets and blanket were folded tidily upon it. The guitars and the banjo and the cello stood undisturbed in their stands, the keyboard and speakers and mixing board unplugged.

She wondered if it brought any solace to her, this space, which she had always found at once comforting and mysterious, the way it smelled of him and mildew and rosin and coffee and Scotch and laundry detergent and spiders.

She wondered if she had slept at all, or if she had just been being polite when she accepted the linens and clothing passed down the concrete stairs last night.

"You came," Moll observed, remaining seated on the dusty rug.

Molly bristled. The words, which should have evoked her pity, which should have exposed to her a heartsick woman waiting apprehensive in darkness, instead evoked only irritation. She considered not speaking. She considered refusing to go through with it. She imagined buying a padlock for the bulkhead doors, entrapping and starving her adversary. But then she felt, like an actual finger pointing, Moll's calculating gaze on her forehead.

"He's in his high chair," Molly said, untying the belt of her blue robe and starting to pull off her pajama pants. "I gave her a pile of Cheerios to feed him one by one."

She stripped down to her underwear. Moll followed suit, removing the old sweatpants and T-shirt that neither of them would ever miss from the messy bottom drawer of the dresser. They swapped clothing and redressed quickly. Molly stole a glance at Moll's body. She couldn't tell if Moll (she) was attractive or not.

The basement was cool but the clothes were warm from Moll. Molly disliked the warmth.

Her phone, in the pocket of the robe lying on the floor between them, began to buzz. They both reached for it. Moll fell back and allowed

Molly to scramble, searching for the phone in one pocket before locating it in the other. David, requesting a video chat. *Decline.*

Molly kept the phone, and the keys from the same pocket, but handed the robe to Moll. They both shivered. Molly found it ominous, that simultaneous shiver.

"So go," Molly said curtly.

Moll hesitated.

"Go," she repeated, unsure how long her vexation, her rage, could hold before giving way to tears.

"So I'll do all of today, through bedtime," Moll said, "and then you can do late tonight and tomorrow before and after work, and I'll do tomorrow night."

Molly couldn't tell whether this was a question or a declaration, but the swiftness of Moll's words, their practiced casualness, indicated that she had carefully prepared this proposition, had rehearsed it many times over.

How about you do none of it? Molly thought. *How about let's not and say we did?*

It took her a second to understand that the source of the heat was blood.

Molly half nodded, a gesture that could perhaps be interpreted as compliance.

Still Moll hesitated.

"Go," Molly said again. She thought of the children, alone at the table.

"I should have the phone," Moll said.

She was right. She should have the phone. The ability to call 911 or anything else.

"And," Moll added, "the wallet."

The wallet, the phone—not *your wallet, your phone.*

Yet she was not wrong.

Molly handed her the phone, careful to avoid contact with her fingers. "The wallet's in the bag," she said. "Hanging on the bedroom door-knob." Shaken, for she had done it too, unintentionally: *the bag,* not *my bag.* "And my keys—" she began, about to hand them over, before remembering that the one thing Moll had was the keys.

"Turn on a lamp," Moll said. "It'll be dark in here when I close the bulkhead."

"She needs her prunes," Molly said. "At least two. And he'll need a nap at—"

"I know," Moll said.

Molly's face felt hot, stung.

Rather than waiting for Molly to follow her advice, Moll walked a few steps to turn on the standing lamp. Then she ran up the steep stairs.

The metal doors crashed together behind her.

Molly turned off the standing lamp.

The blackness of the basement was disrupted only by the faintest gray rectangle of outside light.

2

The metal doors were still reverberating against each other when Molly ran up the stairs and reopened them.

She would not.

She would not.

She would not rot in the basement.

She caught a glimpse of the edge of the blue robe as Moll stepped through the back door into the living room. So she was already inside. Out of reach, in the children's domain. She could no longer be stopped, clawed, dragged to the ground.

"Twenty-three," Molly heard Viv saying loudly before the door slammed shut.

She stood barefoot in the wet grass in her untended backyard, an intruder on her own property. She made her way into the evergreen bush. It must have rained in the night; each needle bore a droplet, and each droplet rolled down onto her, a private storm.

At the table, Viv stood on a chair, on tiptoes, conveying a single Cheerio toward Ben on her flat palm. When the Cheerio was almost close enough for him to touch it, she jerked her hand out of his reach, which was, to him, hilarious.

Moll, it seemed, had not yet spoken to them. She hung back, beside the door, watching them as Molly was watching them.

Molly's heartbeat drew attention to itself.

Would they accept Moll, or would they deny her?

Molly didn't know which possibility caused her greater dread.

Moll appeared unable to step forth into the room.

"Aren't you so glad toothbrushes are alive?" Viv said, her uninhibited voice perfectly audible through the half-open window. "If they weren't alive then we'd all have such brown teeth, right?"

Viv didn't even glance over at Moll, who seemed to be relying on the wall to remain upright.

"Mommy?" Viv said. "Right?" Still she didn't look at Moll; she was busy revoking a Cheerio from Ben.

Moll pressed herself off the wall and walked toward the table.

"Right," she said to Viv, the word little more than a breath. "But actually toothbrushes aren't alive," Moll continued, her voice stronger with each syllable.

"Oh." Viv looked at the bowl of fruit on the table. "Are those apples alive?"

"No. Well, yes. I don't know. Kind of."

Finally Viv, laughing, looked at Moll.

"Mama, don't you know things?"

"Ba wa," Ben demanded, antsy in his high chair.

Molly had the urge to run inside and translate Ben's request for Moll, but Moll was already moving toward the kitchen to fill a bottle with water for him.

She caressed his shoulder as she passed him.

It was an injury, a sizzle on her own palm, the sight of Moll touching her son's body.

Moll returned with the bottle; so eager was Ben that he grabbed the nipple with his teeth when it was still at a sharp angle, which forced him to strain upward like a gerbil as he drank.

"Hey gerbil," Moll said.

"Why gerbil?" Viv said.

"Gerbils' water bottles are mounted on the sides of their cages so they have to drink like this."

"What's a gerbil?"

"Come on, B, let go for a sec, then you can hold it yourself." Moll wrenched the bottle out from between his teeth and handed it to him.

"What's a gerbil?"

Moll twisted her body away from the table, away from Viv's question, and stared directly at Molly in her hiding place inside the bush.

Molly realized, with a chill, that Moll had hidden in the same spot plenty of times.

"Go," Moll mouthed at her, ferocious.

"What, Mommy? What?" Viv said.

"What what?" Moll said, turning back to the table, the savagery vanished from her tone.

"What's a gerbil?"

3

Because the basement wasn't soundproof, David couldn't record if anyone was upstairs. The microphone would capture the sound of the kids running around, the tone of their conversations.

But today Molly was thankful for the basement's penetrability. She listened: their footsteps, their voices, the rhythms of their interactions. She understood, or believed she understood, everything: now someone was hurrying to the bathroom (Viv), now someone (Moll) was offering someone something, now someone (Ben) thumped hard against something and began to scream, now someone (Moll) rushed to him, now someone (Moll, carrying Ben) walked to the children's room (to nurse), now someone (Viv) called for help (couldn't reach the toilet paper).

And so. An average Sunday morning. Buffeted between their needs.

But after a while she came to wish the basement were soundproof. It was too much, the tenor of Moll's voice, the way it successfully placated them. The mutual, palpable bliss of mother and children.

The infinite patience of the mother who was incapable of taking them for granted.

Pained, Molly pulled a pair of David's headphones over her ears to block it all.

She felt uneasy without her phone.

There were plenty of books in the basement, books she wanted to read but never had time to; she often told David that her fantasy was to go to a cabin by herself for a week and read novels for six hours a day. But when she opened one such book and began to read, she felt almost illiterate: she read the same sentence over and over again until the words collapsed into letters and the letters collapsed into lines and circles.

She tried to remember what the kids had been wearing that Friday two weeks ago when Erika brought them to meet her after work. Perhaps Viv had been wearing the jean dress and Ben the yellow sweatshirt. She could picture them in those clothes, heading into the Phillips 66 with Erika. But she didn't know for sure. What she did know was that the jean dress was at this moment hanging in the children's closet, that the yellow sweatshirt (blueberry-stained) was dangling over the side of the laundry hamper.

She yanked off the headphones.

Upstairs, the energy was moving toward the front door, the jitter of feet near the hall closet. Then, the front door opened. Molly shut the book and stepped over the accusatory pile of laundry beside the washing machine in order to reach the end of the basement directly beneath the hall closet.

The front door closed. The house was silent. They were gone; they had gone out.

She was livid. Moll had taken them out without asking her.

Though she well knew that by 9:00 a.m. on a Sunday, some kind of outing was essential.

She should follow them. She would follow them.

She could not be asked to bear this unbearable situation.

She leaned against the cold concrete wall of the basement. Tired. So tired. She had not slept well last night, not on her makeshift bed of blankets in the hallway outside the children's room, not with Moll down here glowing or glowering in her basement.

That viciousness in Moll's eyes. The threat of the word *Go*.

Molly stepped away from the wall, dizzy with the double speeds of Earth, one thousand miles per hour, sixty-seven thousand miles per hour. She wilted onto the futon and realized it would be a very long time before she would have the wherewithal to stand up again.

From this position, with the right side of her face heavy on the mattress, she had a close-up view of the plastic chair with metal legs where David often sat to play.

She considered her reflection in metal legs, her stretched-out alien face. The light from the lamp appeared in the metal legs as four dashes of brilliance; she was outlandish amid the brilliance.

Later, she woke to witness the plastic chair: expectant. Nothing can look as empty as a piece of furniture intended to house the human body.

She remembered, for the first time in a long time, an old fear of hers from when Viv was newborn: that she would go into the baby's room in the morning after letting her cry herself back to sleep in the night only to find an empty crib with a scribble of blood on the sheet, identical to the scribble of blood where a mouse thrashed its way out of the trap on the concrete floor of the basement of her childhood home.

She reached to turn off the lamp. In the dark, a woman walked past the futon. And then another. And another. And another. One after the other after the other after the other after the other.

4

When she again woke, there was once more the jitter of feet near the hall closet, the front door opening, as though no time had passed; as though she had, for hours now, remained stuck in the same instant.

But when she located the alarm clock in the mess of David's stuff beneath the futon and the flashing red numerals yielded the time (3:37), she understood that Ben had recently woken from his nap, that they were now headed out for the requisite second outing of Sunday.

The front door slammed; she pictured Viv pulling it shut with all her might.

She ran up the basement stairs, pressed through the metal doors (not padlocked from the outside), emerged unsteady into the luminous afternoon. She tried opening the back door. It was negligent of Moll to have forgotten to lock it, but she was glad to save the seconds it would have taken her to use the key.

She slipped into her home (just as messy as it would have been under her watch at this hour on a Sunday; dishes on the table, toys everywhere).

In the bedroom she opened her closet. She didn't have time to change out of the sweatpants and T-shirt into more reasonable clothing. She shoved her feet into sneakers and ran out the front door.

They were not visible from the front steps. They had made good time, already turning left or right at the sidewalk and then left or right at the corner. Sometimes it took ten minutes just to get from the front steps to the stop sign. She guessed that they had turned left and left again, on their way to the playground and the old carousel, which was open only on Sundays. At least, that's what she would have done with them today, which either did or did not mean that Moll would do the same. She ran. Left, and left again.

There they were. Their three bodies of such different sizes, moving slowly down the sidewalk together. So this was what she and her children looked like from behind.

Perhaps they had made good time for the first block and a half, but no longer. Viv wanted to push the stroller rather than ride in it; she kept steering it off the sidewalk, veering onto people's front yards. Ben was walking, dawdling, gripping Moll's finger. Molly never would have permitted him to walk at this juncture; far too far to go. She knew he must have squirmed so much in the baby carrier that Moll, tenderer than she, had released him from his entrapment.

Molly considered the other baby carrier, the

matching carrier in Moll's world. The same tan color, the same watermelon stain.

The thought caused her to hang back like a guest at a funeral. She kept a safe distance, moving from tree to tree, relieved at the abandoned quality of these particular blocks on Sunday afternoon.

"Is that cat dead?" she was close enough to hear Viv say when they passed the veterinarian's office.

"No," Moll said, lifting a surprisingly compliant Ben and inserting him into the carrier with practiced grace.

"Excuse me," Viv said to the fire hydrant into which she rammed the stroller.

Instants later, Molly too passed the window where the calico cat slept a deathlike sleep on the desk.

5

"Seven," Moll and Viv shouted together. "Eight. Nine. Ten. Eleven. Twelve."

At each odd number, Moll pushed Viv's swing with her right hand. At each even number, she pushed Ben's swing with her left hand. This method Molly had developed for pushing both at once had always felt to her like a literalization of the phrase *she's got her hands full.*

Molly sat with her back up against a tree, facing away from the playground that was uninhabited aside from them, listening to herself and her daughter count to one hundred.

Fifty-three (Viv), fifty-four (Ben), fifty-five (Viv), fifty-six (Ben), fifty-seven (Viv), fifty-eight (Ben), fifty-nine (Viv), sixty (Ben) . . .

For Moll, though, the numbers were not a slog. There was joy in her voice.

Later Viv was going down the slide and Moll was nursing Ben on a sun-soaked bench. Molly's glimpse of the scene made her aware of the weight of her own milk. Her need for relief. He was hungry, urgent, embracing the other woman with every part of his body. They sat as one in the sun: the extreme heat of the mother, the extreme heat of the nursing baby, the furnace of the universe.

Molly peeked around the tree, her face wet. She knew she ought to be more careful, keep herself better hidden, shield herself from Moll's rage, protect her children from the sight of two mothers.

Eventually Ben fell away from the breast and Moll refastened herself. But their intimacy did not end there. He was holding his squeaky giraffe and it seemed that he wished for Moll to bite it. Molly would have refused to let him put it in her mouth, but Moll accepted the giraffe's head and bit until it squeaked. Ben had never seen anything so amusing. He bit and squeaked the legs of the giraffe. She bit and squeaked the giraffe's head. He bit, she bit, on and on, excruciating.

Viv was nowhere to be seen. She was not on the slide. She was not climbing the ladder. She was not reaching for the monkey bars.

She was weaving among the trees, picking things up off the ground, getting closer and closer to Molly. Molly inched around the tree trunk, out of view.

"Mommy?" Viv said, sounding just slightly lost. "Mom?"

Molly waited for Moll to say something, to call out to Viv, "Over here!"

But she didn't.

And Molly was suddenly appalled at herself: she had handed her children over to a woman mangled by grief. There was no way such a mother could do all that needed to be done.

"I got treasures," Viv said, veering back toward the playground.

"Oh, show me!" Moll cried out then from the bench.

As Moll examined the bits of glittering litter in Viv's hands, Molly left them. She would go home and shut herself up in the basement until nightfall. She would prepare the right words to cast Moll out of her life forever.

Yet approaching the perimeter of the park, she found herself unable to exit. She sprinted back to the playground.

They were gone. Afternoon was shading into night. Maybe they had gone home along a different path. But then she heard the distant insistent tinkle and clang.

Moll stood out from afar, wearing her favorite sweatshirt, encircling her son with both arms, stationed between the pair of unreal-colored horses that carried her children into the falling darkness. Each time they went around it seemed that they were riding off into the shadows, but of course they kept circling back, again and again, protected always by the rows of merry lights.

The children's faces were wondrous, ecstatic, but Moll looked solemn, straight-necked, almost ceremonial, as though she bore the world atop her orbiting body.

6

Often there were spiders in the metal sink in the half bath in the basement. Her unneeded milk hissed against the metal and riveleted down the sides toward the black hole of the drain. Her wrists ached.

It was getting harder by the minute, each second a wound.

Her body could not contain this longing.

Maybe if she sat. Maybe if she just sat silently on the rug, waiting. Cross-legged.

Time would pass over and around her.

Time would, eventually, deliver them to her.

Would deliver her to the moment in which she articulated her refusal.

Unless—unless— (the possibility of which she declined to contemplate.)

Only after a while did it dawn on her that she was sitting on the rug in the exact same location and position as Moll had been when she came down to the basement this morning.

Yet she did not move. She sat.

A few decades of silence.

Then, that scrape of steel on brick.

Moll came down the steep stairs. Her body rigid, her expression cold.

Molly felt feverish, spastic, in comparison.

"Don't ever follow me again," Moll said, "or I will kill you."

There was a glint in her eye—sarcasm or menace? The hint of a more direct reckoning, a convenient disappearance (the outskirts of town, those sparse desolate groves) followed by the seamless insertion of herself into Molly's life?

Molly's struggle to decipher Moll's tone caused her own anguish to lose its focus. She imagined what she herself would be capable of, if; the thought shook her and she had to shake it off.

"Are they asleep?" Molly said.

Moll nodded.

"We shouldn't be down here," Molly said. Viv often woke in the early hours of the night, thirsty and scared, needing a mother.

Moll nodded again.

Molly led the way up the stairs and out the bulkhead. Moll stood on the grass, unhelpful, while Molly heaved the metal doors shut.

"The blinds," Moll said flatly when they were both in the living room, the back door locked behind them. She watched as Molly pulled down all the blinds until they were protected from outside eyes.

Moll settled onto the couch, put her feet up on

the coffee table where she had hidden when she was a deer, focused her gaze on Molly.

"So," Moll said, a statement or a question.

This was the time to use the words that would cast Moll out of her life forever.

And she searched, she searched, but she could not quite find the right words.

The unassailable argument against their arrangement—it eluded her.

The phone buzzed in the pocket of the sweatshirt Moll was wearing. She pulled it out and handed it to Molly. David, again; *Decline,* again. Poor David. But she could not answer the phone, could not speak to him; not with Moll's eyes drilling into her.

"Seventh time today," Moll said.

Molly was struck, for the first time, by the thought of Moll's David, in Moll's world, the grieving David, and it sickened her.

She felt guilty toward her own David, and missed him, but the emotions were distant, misty, as though they belonged to someone else.

"We'll tell him in person," Moll said. "Once he's back. In six days."

Molly stiffened, alarmed. Tell him? Tell him—what?

Down the hallway, the children's doorknob began to turn, the well-known squeak.

They darted in different directions, Moll into the bathtub, pulling the shower curtain shut behind her, Molly into the bedroom, into the darkness of the mirrored closet.

Viv, coming down the hall. That slight damp quality of her bare feet on the wood.

"I'm scared from my dream," Viv said to the empty kitchen, the empty couch.

Her footsteps became hastier, panicked.

Molly emerged from the dark closet into the dark bedroom, feeling her daughter's panic as though it were her own (was it?), desperate to arrive at the instant a few seconds from now when she would be holding Viv close, reunited, the comfort of the home reasserting itself.

But Viv had gone into the bathroom. And now the sound of the shower curtain being pulled to the side. So it was Moll who enveloped Viv, Moll whose body cast Viv's nightmare out of the house.

Molly couldn't hear Moll's words, too low and quiet, but she could hear Viv's as she tiptoed past the bathroom, toward the back door, the night, the basement, her unplanned banishment: ". . . you playing hide-and-seek with me? . . . Juice . . . Okay fine water . . . a worm as big as a moon . . ."

7

She waited for Moll, praying that she would honor her own proposed schedule and swap Molly in as soon as she got Viv back to sleep.

She thought of the spiders all around her, maybe crawling up her.

She cursed Moll. She felt as though she had not touched their bodies in weeks.

She had the phone now. She could call someone. 911, or Erika, or David.

She thought of what she could do to Moll. With what household implements.

She horrified herself. She tried to soothe herself by turning her thoughts to other things: to visions of round, smooth surfaces. The image of a wooden bowl. The image of a sand dune. The image of Ben's forehead. But any serene image, she realized, bore within itself the opposite of serenity, the possibility of the shattering of the surface.

The screech of the doors woke her. It was morning, white and damp. She was sprawled messily on the futon. Her vision was blurry with sleep and lack of sleep.

"I fell asleep when I was putting her down," Moll said. "I woke up just now."

Molly pretended it was a lie, though she knew it wasn't—how many times had it happened to her, the tendrils of her child's sleep gripping at her, tying her to the little bed?

"Are they awake?"

"Not yet."

Moll settled herself onto her spot on the worn rug, cross-legged and grave, as though she had no intention of moving a muscle for the next twelve hours, her docility at once reassuring and unsettling.

Upstairs, Molly locked the back door behind her. The home was silent with the silence of sleeping children. She went into the bathroom—when had she last cleaned herself?—and shed the stupid T-shirt and sweatpants, and turned the shower on, very hot, and stood under it for a while, but not too long, because they would be up any second.

It was strange to see strands of dark hair in the bathtub drain and not know if they were hers or hers.

She pulled the towel off the hook (had she pulled this towel off this hook?). She was half-dry when Ben called for her. She swooped him out of the crib and onto her big bed, where, finally, so warm, that heat of him, he nursed, at first frenetic and then indifferent, sucking lazily, detaching.

Now Viv was up, jumping on the bed, jumping on them, and Molly was in the chaos of it, the impeccable chaos, while two yards below a woman sat in the dark.

"Too tight!" Viv cried out. "Let me go!" And Ben, also, following his sister's lead, writhed out of Molly's grasp.

Usually they felt endless, these mornings alone with the kids, the minutes unreliable, expanding infinitely, but today two hours felt like a few moments, and then Erika was coming through the door.

"Happy Monday!" Erika very nearly shouted as she entered. "Well Miss Viv, I hear there was an exceptionally beautiful fish at your party." Erika winked at Molly, who couldn't bring herself to wink back.

She ought to send Erika home, call in sick to work, spend the whole day with the kids, maybe pack them into the car and drive away forever.

But she had to go to work. It was even more important that she go to work.

"Of course," Viv said. She was on the rug, stuck beneath Ben, who was trying to lick her eye. She was having fun with him and then she wasn't. "Get him off me!"

Erika picked him up and smeared kisses across his forehead. Molly got a pang, watching another woman kiss her boy, but it wasn't Erika's fault.

"Mommy, since Ben licked my eye, can I lick your eye?"

"No," Molly said.

"Please?" Viv said. "You'll like it."

"Your saliva might sting my eye."

"It what?" Viv was distraught.

"Just kidding."

"So I can lick your eye?"

"No. Get your backpack. We're almost late."

On their walk to the car—a block and a half away, the nearest parking spot she could find upon their return from the dangerous frolic in the median a hundred years ago—Viv gripped her hand, and Molly could feel the stretching of her daughter's tendons. She brought her awareness, too much awareness, to the union of their hands, until she felt Viv's heartbeat in her palm like a thing she was holding.

She jerked her hand out of Viv's.

"Excuse me," Viv said to a puddle, jumping over it, unbothered.

They were stopped at the first red light when Viv said, from her car seat in the back, "Once upon a time we went to the carousel yesterday."

The light turned green.

"Right, Mom?"

"That's right," Molly said.

But Viv was in a great mood and did not notice the tightness in her mother's voice.

"I can't believe I'm four," she said.

"Do you like being four?"

"I love it. But also I want to be five and six and eight and nine and stuff."

"Why?"

"I want to get older so I can be a mommy."

"Yes, I had to get old enough," Molly said, resisting the urge to correct Viv, to say that she should look forward to being older so she could be a scientist or artist or president as well as a mother. "So that I could be yours."

"Yes," Viv said, "because I was waiting for you."

"You were waiting for me?"

"Yes."

"Where were you waiting for me?"

"Everywhere."

8

She needed to be the first to arrive at work, and, thanks to driving too fast after dropping off Viv at school, here she was, in the empty parking lot. She ran toward the Phillips 66, key chain in hand, overwhelmed by the sensation of being chased, though the parking lot couldn't have been more peaceful.

A scattering of birds, no wind.

She used the thickest key to open the front door of the display room. It was dim and still, smelling of dust and fossils and old coffee, as always. She flicked the lights: the noise of the fluorescence.

How innocent the Bible looked, there in its glass case; undisturbed, undisturbing.

She ran through the glass door that led from the display room to the offices and lab. The cardboard box where she had initially gathered the artifacts was still there, in the shadows beneath her desk.

She grabbed the box and returned to the display room and used the smallest key to unlock the glass case bearing the Bible. Then she unlocked the glass case containing the other objects.

Gingerly, she placed the Coca-Cola bottle, the Altoids tin, the potsherd, and the toy soldier in the cardboard box with the Bible.

She was stupid to have shared them. She should have hidden them all away.

She remembered the day, only a month ago, when she had perused the Bible cover to cover to confirm that every single mention of God was feminized.

Molly carried the box back to her cubicle and pushed it as far under her desk as possible.

Now she felt a little bit safe. She was, she realized, breathing hard.

Then she remembered that there was a sixth object. The penny she had found in the Pit and quickly dismissed—the penny from Moll's world.

She remembered change scattering out of her pocket as she slid to the bottom of the Pit, laden. She remembered a penny in the mud. Her daughter is always on the lookout for pennies, heads up for good luck.

But where was that penny now?

In Molly's wallet, still, probably, where she had dropped it along with the control penny on Friday.

She pulled her wallet out of her bag. She felt as though she could sense the penny in there, burning with its otherness, the change purse suddenly toxic.

She dumped the coins out onto her desk and pulled all six pennies toward her. There were only two possible contenders, as only two had been minted in the current year. One penny belonging to her, one belonging to Moll. But there was nothing to distinguish them from each other. She found herself wishing for a hint, some telltale sign (a fleck of blood?) so that she could know which penny was the dangerous one—and then was horrorstruck by her wish.

She tossed both pennies into the cardboard box along with the other objects and tried to forget about them.

The Phillips 66 felt acutely abandoned. She kept having the sensation that this wasn't quite the same workplace she had left on Friday. It was always odd to reemerge from the fog of the weekend into work on Monday mornings, but today it was a hundred times so. She questioned every object—the dimensions of her desk, the hue of her chair, the angle of her computer monitor.

She turned the computer on. She had to write a notice for today's tourists. And then would borrow the language from that to write a press release. And then would send it to all the relevant news outlets.

As she waited for her computer to awaken, she began to compose the letter in her head: *Dear Tourists*. But that sounded off somehow. *Dear*

Customers? Dear Guests? Dear Enthusiasts? Dear People? To Whom It May Concern? Her mind was too frenetic. She could sort out the salutation later. *It has come to our attention that the artifacts that have been (lately? recently? in recent times?) discovered at our site alongside our (notable? noteworthy? legendary?) fossils are, in fact, as originally suspected by many, a hoax . . . an elaborate hoax . . . please forgive our . . . when initially unearthed, these objects defied our understanding, but . . . it has been proven beyond a doubt . . . with 100 percent confidence . . . with absolute certainty . . . after consultation with (multiple? numerous?) experts . . . have been found to be . . . including, most significantly, the Bible . . . we hope you can forgive . . . upon this revelation, were immediately removed from the eye of the public . . . the thorny road of truth . . . the thorny path of science . . . the . . . the . . .*

The computer screen, now bright, confronted her with the photograph: the kids hugging each other, wearing adult backpacks and fearful expressions.

She couldn't last a minute with those four eyes on her.

She had to get rid of the picture before doing anything else. She clicked on her desktop settings and began scrolling through the ravishing stock images: a waterfall cascading through ferns,

222

a beach under a red sun, a forest of aspen and columbine.

"Molly!" Corey startled her. She had been absorbed in toggling back and forth between the waterfall and the forest.

"Hey," she said. He had yanked aside the curtain in the doorway.

"We have to call the police."

"Why?"

"Someone broke in. The cases are open. The Bible and everything is gone."

"No," Molly said. "I have it all. Right here."

"Oh." He gave a quick laugh. "Okay. Good. Shit. I was freaking out."

"I don't think we should display them anymore."

"What?"

She didn't know what to tell him or not tell him.

"Molly?" he said.

"The culprit," Roz said dryly, appearing in the doorway behind him.

Corey looked at Molly, waited for her to speak.

"Molly doesn't want to display the Bible anymore," Corey said.

"Abandoning your pet project?" Roz said.

Molly loved these two, her dear colleagues, wry Roz and kind Corey, but right now they seemed somehow different to her, capable of unpleasantness.

223

"Think of the ticket sales," Corey said.

She was sitting and they were standing. She disliked this difference in her position and theirs. She stood.

"What about all the hate mail?" Molly said.

"What about it?" Roz said.

"Getting used to it," Corey said.

"What if someone—"

"Like what," Roz said, "like some kind of religious extremist shooter or something?"

Molly didn't know whether to be comforted or frightened by Roz's immediate understanding.

"Well," Roz said, "*vivir con miedo es vivir a medias*."

"What?" Corey said.

"A life lived in fear is a life half-lived," Molly translated. "But I have kids."

"I'll put the stuff back in the cases," Roz said.

"No." Molly should have taken the Bible off-site, destroyed it, thrown it in the reservoir.

"Come on, Molly," Corey said.

"No," she said.

"I insist." Roz could be fierce, and she was becoming fierce.

"It's dangerous," Molly said. "I had a—"

"A what?"

Molly couldn't say it.

"A what?" Roz insisted.

"A dream," Molly said, backing down.

"Of?"

"A bomber. My children—"

"Oh, your kids," Corey said, kind again. "Oh, poor Molly."

"Yes, poor Molly," Roz said. "But a dream is a dream is a dream."

"Well," Molly said, at a loss, "it didn't feel like a dream."

"Well, sometimes they don't," Roz said. "So, hand it over."

"Fine," Molly said, brashness rising in her, "but if you display it, then I refuse to give any tours."

How could she give a tour, every woman in a baseball cap a possible bomber?

"Okay," Corey said. "Okay, that's fine. You can do excavation today."

But she couldn't go into the Pit, sacrifice herself to the vagaries of a seam that might spit her out into a reality where her children were dead or whatever else. How ridiculous that she had ever taken comfort in the Pit, had ever leaned against its dirt wall and appreciated its solidity— the treacherous, porous Pit.

She was running so fast to get them away and then she ran over the edge of the Pit and they sort of fell down into it, the three of them, his body in her right arm and her body in her left arm, slipping and scooting down the mud, and because they were not laughing, she knew.

"Or," Corey added, looking closely at her face, "you can do desk duty for now. I was going to

225

update the website with the new schedule and file the hate mail and tabulate ticket sales and proofread the grant proposal."

"No one should be giving tours," Molly said. "No one should be excavating."

"Okay," Roz said, reaching under Molly's desk to grab the box. "See you guys."

Molly could feel her adrenaline draining away, leaving her feeble, empty. She didn't even try to stop Roz.

"God," Corey said, "do I seriously hear a tour bus already?"

After he was gone, she toggled back and forth between the desktop images for another long while before settling on the forest.

Then she began to type the hoax announcement. But her fingers didn't work well on the keyboard; the words came too slowly, refused to blend into sentences.

After a while she had to give up.

She sat numb at her desk. Her milk came down but she did not pump. She thought of Moll in the basement. Wondered if her milk too had come down. If she was at this moment squeezing it out into the metal sink.

She was interrupted by Corey, dropping off a pile of hate mail for her to sort. He didn't say anything, just placed the mail on her desk and shot her a sympathetic look on his way out.

The top postcard bore a Renaissance painting

of Mary nursing Jesus, a surprisingly graphic portrait: both her nipple and his penis were exposed. Molly turned it over. No return address. Just a single word in graceful handwriting: *See?*

The word set off a physical reaction in her: a wavering of her vision, a weakening of her muscles.

She put the postcard down atop the other mail, the white envelopes that looked venomous in their similarity and anonymity, American flag stamps and blue ballpoint ink, implying all the typical sentiments contained within: *UNDO THIS HORRIFIC SIN OR YOU WILL BE PUNISHED. GOD IS DISPLEASED. HE IS ENRAGED. YOU ARE ON A COLLISION COURSE WITH GOD AND HIS FAITHFUL CHILDREN. BEWARE THE BLINDING LIGHT. HE ALWAYS KNOWS WHERE YOU ARE.*

She needed to get away from it. She needed to be around people. Corey, Roz. She burst out of her cubicle. She could see through the glass door that Corey was in the display room, in the middle of his tour.

There were three thirtysomething women on the tour, one of them wearing jeans and a sweatshirt, and as much as she wanted to run in there and save Corey, her body moved her back to her cubicle, into the dark space beneath her desk.

Her phone buzzed in her pocket and she answered it accidentally, her finger's swipe to decline the video call landing on the wrong part of the phone's surface.

"Where are you?" David said.

She crawled out from under her desk.

"Were you under your desk?"

"Cords," she said.

His face looked distant in the small window. It calmed her to see him, but the calmness was fleeting, almost immediately overthrown by despair. She wished that her life hadn't changed. That she could be at peace, briefly video-chatting with her wondrous husband during her engaging workday while her children thrived and napped.

"Molly?"

She tried to think of how to talk to him; if she told him anything right now, she feared it would come out as a scream.

"Molly." His voice was accusatory. "Where were you guys yesterday? Why didn't you pick up ever?"

"At the carousel." It sounded thin; she could hear how thin it sounded.

A few beats passed between them. She wanted to tell him everything. She wanted them to be united, all-powerful, capable of ejecting Moll from their lives. The fantasy spiraled quickly, absurdly—superhero masks and capes, lightning bolts shooting out of their fingers; Moll shocked, meek, terrified, slinking away forever.

"What the fuck is going on, Molly?"

She was disturbed by the image of Moll that had sprung up in her mind, Moll reduced and pitiful; the words from the song David sang so well came to her, *burned out from exhaustion, buried in the hail, poisoned in the bushes and blown out on the trail, hunted like a crocodile, ravaged in the corn.*

"I'm burned out from exhaustion," she borrowed.

"Buried in the hail," he said, without missing a beat, and she loved him.

It was he who had stood in the doorway the same day as the car accident and said *What the hell, let's have a kid.* Molly remembered the ensuing sex, how directly it had led to Viv, how urgent it had been, sex following a car accident in which people could have been hurt but no one was hurt.

"I'm sorry," she said, straining to hear Corey droning on, still alive.

"Molly?" he implored. "Molly?"

She thought of Moll. Of Moll's David.

"Later," she promised. "Soon. I'm at work."

He stared at her through the screen. She looked away from the screen.

"I'm going to call you tonight," he said finally. "And if you don't pick up—"

He hung up. She sat in her chair. She stared at the list of website updates Corey had emailed her. She looked at the black letters on the screen, trying to see the pixels.

It was long and not long before a text message dinged into her phone: Erika.

Hey is it really true that Viv can get pizza dough to play with if we swing by the back door before the pizza place opens?

The question pulled Molly back into her life: her life, the delight of it all, all the things that made you forget you were hurtling through space moving two colossal speeds at once, the precious guys at the pizza place with their accents and generosity.

Yeah Viv sometimes dies! she texted back.

It took her an instant to notice the typo.

DOES, she corrected.

But the damage was done. The catastrophic typo. She had to get home to them.

9

Waiting at the light to turn right off the thorough-fare, she couldn't believe she was already almost home; couldn't recall a single second of her drive. That bizarre thing of getting in the car and then arriving at your destination with no memory of what had passed around you.

But here she was, 4:23 p.m. She rolled down all four windows, inviting in the wind. Erika always took Ben in the stroller to walk Viv home from school; probably they had returned ten or fifteen minutes ago. It would be so fun to surprise them, to seize them both and spin them around and dazzle them with her presence. To let Erika go an hour and a half early but still pay her the full amount.

They were always desperate for her by this time of day. And she was desperate for them. The desire manifested itself physically, an actual itch at her wrist, an actual ache when she breathed in: the need for their bodies.

She heard them (their unmistakable screeches, their stabs of laughter) an instant before she spotted them. They must be out front with Erika.

She got closer. They were in the front yard. But not with Erika.

She was spinning them, had seized them up, was spinning both of them at once.

10

There was nothing to do but glide past them unnoticed, for they were caught up in their ecstatic dizziness.

There was nothing to do but park the car on a different block and sneak through backyards toward the evergreen bush. Nothing to do but let her mute rage accumulate.

She could call Erika, explain everything, get Erika on board. *That woman wasn't me,* she would say. *We're going to fucking save these amazing kids,* Erika would say, swearing to be at Molly's side *ASAP.* Or, Erika would be initially amused, thinking it a joke, and then deeply concerned about Molly's mental health.

When Molly reached her own backyard, Moll and the children were still out front. Talking with affable Capria Lewis, their neighbor from half a block down. Who was confused.

"But you were in the car," Capria Lewis said.

"The car?" Moll said.

So it was Capria who would call them out, who would shatter their flimsy, reckless arrangement.

"I was—" Capria said, "you were—but now you're—"

"Do you have lollipops," Viv wanted to know.

"Do you have a toothbrush," Capria rejoined, their habitual exchange.

"Thank you," Viv said, and, "Say 'Thank you,' B."

"Well I guess I'm just getting old," Capria said insincerely.

"Hey look!" Viv yelled, and they all moved to the other side of the front yard, and Molly could no longer hear them.

She felt like an intruder, crouching in the evergreen bush, catapulted out of her life, transformed into someone with nothing. She tried to shake the feeling. She reminded herself that no neighbor would ever call the police to tell them that Molly had been seen stalking around her own backyard.

When after too long they came into the house through the front door, Viv was saying, "—spell Molly?"

"Actually," Moll said, "a lot like the way you spell Mommy. But with *L*s rather than *M*s."

"L-O-L-L-Y?"

They all went into the bathroom together and closed the door. Molly strained but could hear nothing.

After a while they emerged from the bathroom. Ben wasn't wearing pants or a diaper. *He ought to be wearing a diaper,* Molly thought. *Go to the bedroom and get him a diaper.* But Moll went to the kitchen.

From inside the bush, Molly bore witness to Moll's comfort as she rinsed the carrots, as she grated the cheese, as she instructed Viv to choose napkins, as she slid the quesadillas into the toaster: a woman rushing around her kitchen, her life, in motion and at peace, erasing that other universe with her every gesture, the infiltration perfecting itself. She wondered if Moll knew or cared that she was there, watching, in the bush.

Ben squatted and pooped on the floor near the table. He stood up and gazed down at it. He knelt to examine it. Molly was about to shout a warning, but Viv beat her to it:

"No B don't!"

Moll sprinted over and grabbed him an instant before his fingers sank in.

Ben chortled as Moll lifted him above her head.

"No!" Viv said. "Don't laugh when you make a problem, B."

The combination of his sister's distressed face and his mother's distressed face was more than he could bear. He launched himself to the height of a scream with no warm-up.

"He should have been wearing a diaper," Viv chided.

After a moment Ben stopped crying. Moll cleaned the floor, using wet wipes to scoop the poop into a diaper. The children watched, rapt. Then Moll raced to the kitchen, where (Molly assumed) the quesadillas were starting to burn in the toaster.

This woman, Molly thought, *could burn my house down.*

As though no quesadilla had ever burned under her own watch.

As though she wouldn't have relieved the babysitter and started playing with them before the other mother got home.

Viv said to Ben, "You have a little baby skeleton inside you. Did you know that?"

Ben looked at Viv.

Viv put a yellow blanket over her head and bobbed around the living room, chanting, "The pillows are haunted. The couch is haunted. The rug is haunted."

After a while Ben grew bored of her litany. He wandered into the kitchen and came up behind Moll where she was standing at the sink rinsing grapes. He grabbed her legs to steady himself. Moll reached down and patted his head.

When Moll touched him, Molly experienced the sensation on her own hand.

That feeling of his hair. Outrageously soft.

She extricated herself from the bush. She went to the basement to grieve.

11

In the basement there was a three-foot piece of old metal piping leaned up against the concrete wall behind the guitar stands. It had not been there before. Probably it had been in the basement, somewhere amid the chaos of boxes and junk on the far side. But it had not been on display. Now, it served as proof that Moll did not simply sit all day; that she moved around the cellar, simmering with plans; that she had located at least one weapon.

And, another change from before: in the middle of the futon, awaiting Molly almost like a gift, the spare unit for the baby monitor.

So Moll had been eavesdropping far more profoundly than permitted by the bush. Into the children's bedroom. Why hadn't Molly thought to do the same?

The worn-out spot on the rug pulled her to it. She settled herself there, cross-legged, bereft, enraged, the metal pipe heavy across her thighs, the baby monitor light in her hand. She turned the dial:

"—made of plastic?" Viv was saying. Ben was crying.

"Ceramic," Moll said.

"Wood?" Viv persisted.

Moll soothed Ben.

"Well, wood?"

Ben allowed himself to be soothed.

"Plastic?"

Molly turned off the monitor.

Scornfully she considered herself, her former attitudes and actions. How often had she, naive with privilege, threatened David: *If those kids don't learn to sleep through the night I'm seriously going to move to the basement.*

Time passed the way it passed in the basement: not measureable.

Was this now her life: inside the cellar, outside of time?

Like Moll.

Eons later, Moll opened the metal doors and came down the stairs with a cardboard box.

The basement was dark. Moll turned on a lamp. She did not react when she saw the metal pipe lying across Molly's lap.

Nor did Molly pick it up and use it as she had intended.

When she saw Moll in the lamplight what she saw in the lamplight was herself.

Moll removed things from the box and placed them on the futon: the gray scarf, the blue hoodie, the white T-shirt, the fleece socks. Not even David was aware of her fondness for that particular T-shirt, those particular socks. The most private and mundane of preferences. Known only to her. And to the person who had once owned them, too, elsewhere—the secret softness inside the pockets of the blue hoodie.

"Settling in," Molly observed, trying to sound cold, but her vocal cords were disobedient, her voice the croak of a creature accustomed to darkness.

"Your turn," Moll said.

"Turn," Molly scoffed. Then, "Asleep?"

Moll nodded.

Molly felt depleted, as though it would require superhuman effort to restore herself to sufficient buoyancy to go up the stairs.

She rolled the metal pipe off her legs and stood, with effort.

"Do you feel like you're losing your children?" Moll said.

The audacity of the question.

Molly hissed her response.

"Good!" Moll said, spitting the word out of her mouth like a curse. "Good! Because that's what happened to me."

They were too close to each other, same face to same face, like raging at yourself in the mirror. Molly recalled watching herself cry or laugh in the mirror as a child: observing her face distorted in despair or mirth made her cry or laugh all the harder.

"But your children," Moll said, "are alive and well. Your grief is the tiniest fraction of mine."

Molly envisioned them, smooth, asleep, just a few feet above their heads. She needed to be upstairs, near them, in case.

"You should go upstairs," Moll said.

"We have to find her."

"Her?"

"The bomber. She's dead in your world but not— She was driving a black rental car, I saw it."

"What can we do?" Moll's voice was hollow. "Some woman in a black rental car two weeks ago? There's nothing we can do."

"She could still—" Molly said. "I tried to hide the Bible and the other artifacts but Roz and Corey—"

"Maybe someone killed her children," Moll said.

"What do you mean?" Panic surged through Molly.

"Maybe," Moll said, staring at the cement floor, "when your children are killed, you kill in turn."

Frightened, Molly waited for Moll to say something else.

But Moll was quiet.

"I'm going upstairs," Molly announced, but she did not move toward the stairs.

"When I'm with them," Moll said, "I feel like I

240

never lost them. And I feel like I'm losing them every second."

Molly froze at this confession; found herself, for some reason, remembering the freshness of the amniotic fluid. Whooshing out of her, the cleanest thing she had ever encountered. That otherworldly liquid in which their impeccable bodies had been suspended, safe.

They were already standing so close, but Moll took a step closer, matched her body up to Molly's: thighs to thighs, torso to torso. The slow and hurting beating of her heart. Molly smelled the unwashed smell of herself, doubled, heady. Moll's face drooped onto Molly's neck.

Despite having conceived and borne and birthed and nursed children, this was the most intimate human sensation she had ever experienced: Moll's warm tears moving across the skin of her collarbone.

It was the lightest touch imaginable, traveling downward toward the indentation between her breasts. She found herself opening to it, open to it, this subtlest interplay between two echoing forms.

But it was too much. She needed to step back.

Yet she could not. She was addicted to it, to the movement of the tears, the lack of gaps between them.

After a while Moll pulled her head up off

Molly's neck, revoking the tears, and Molly braced herself for further distancing. But Moll's lips too were parted, and their lips matched themselves up, and their teeth.

12

Upstairs, Molly carried the sleeping children from their room into her bed. It was unwise, disruptive to their rest and to hers, but she needed to sleep, or half sleep, beside them. She needed to look at them and look at them again the whole night long.

She drowsed and woke and drowsed and woke, and, in the in-between states, forgot about Moll and Moll's children—instead was struck, at the sight and sound and smell of her children, by an outlandish joy, its tinge of sorrow momentarily inexplicable to her, until she remembered.

When the sky lightened, she pulled herself away from the meadow of their sleep. She took a shower and dressed for work and pulled open the window beside the evergreen, and then carried her pajamas to the basement. Moll was asleep on the futon, which had been pressed down into its bed form at last, the sheets spread out properly.

Only when Molly saw Moll sleeping there did she realize how much she had been dreading the sight of her sitting stiffly on the worn-out spot, cross-legged and unrested.

Her body still felt to her like an echo of Moll's and when she looked at Moll's body it still felt like an echo of hers.

She perched on the edge of the futon and watched Moll as she had watched her children. This was no meadow. Asleep, Moll's face was still and sad, the menace faded into mournfulness.

13

Ben was eating yogurt naked in his high chair. Viv was jumping naked from the coffee table to the couch. Moll, in Molly's pajamas, moved through the space with the serenity that Molly longed for on these solo mornings of getting the kids ready when David was gone.

Molly watched from inside the evergreen, straining to catch each word through the window she had opened.

"Hey," Viv said (clear, loud), "do you know why I have such a huge belly?"

"No," Moll said, surprising Molly with the flatness of her voice.

"Well actually it's because I'm going to have a baby."

Moll wiped the trail of yogurt off Ben's chin, neck, belly.

"And do you know who that baby is going to be?"

"No." Moll held out a pair of underwear for Viv to step into.

"You. Baby Mommy."

Why wasn't Moll more amused, more vivacious?

"You smell funny," Viv said to Moll. "Why do you smell that way?"

Moll pulled a shirt over Viv's head and said something that Molly couldn't hear.

"Can I lick your eye?" Viv smiled in anticipation of the refusal, the begging.

But Moll nodded and knelt.

"I can?" Viv said with awe.

Molly had to stretch, stand on tiptoe, to witness them together on the floor. Viv put her hands on Moll's cheeks and pulled her close and licked her eye.

"You taste different," Viv said.

"Different from what?" Moll said.

But Viv just laughed.

And then they all left the room, no longer visible from Molly's vantage within the evergreen.

14

Molly pulled open the curtain of her cubicle to find Roz and Corey inside, waiting.

"Where is it?" Roz said.

"It's okay, Molly," Corey said. "Just give it all back."

"Give what back?" she said.

"At least this time you relocked the cases." Roz was at her flintiest.

Molly panicked, wondered: *Moll? The bomber? Some other extremist?*

It *would* have been her, had she gotten the opportunity; that was why she had come to work.

But it had not been her.

"Molly," Corey said gently. "Where are they, dear?" Corey, who, on another Earth, was appearing in newspaper headlines, was being remembered in an obituary. Were the articles mentioning his recent hundred-mile bike ride to raise money for science textbooks in local schools? *Those killed in the blast include . . .*

"I'm not feeling great," Molly said.

"I can tell," Corey said.

"Where's the Bible?" Roz said.

"If we can just get the old girl back on her throne before the tour starts," Corey said. "They're already starting to gather outside. A rather devout-looking group, I'd say."

His jolly declaration chilled her.

"The devout ones are the scary ones," Molly said.

"I guess," he said. "But we know what they're here for, so let's give it to them."

"Are there any women on the tour?" Molly said.

He looked at her funny. "Um, yes."

"Like what age?"

"Molly," Corey said, "whatever this is, it'll pass. I promise. Can you get the things now, please?"

"I don't have them."

The bark that was Roz's laugh. Something about that laugh, its unassailable confidence, set Molly off.

"Where," Molly said, "do you think they come from? All these fossils and the Bible and the rest?"

"From a parallel universe, of course," Roz singsonged.

Roz was joking. But Molly decided to run with it anyway.

"Well, what about it?" she said. "What if the Pit really is some kind of seam where things from other possible worlds come through, like from the world where the Neanderthals didn't go extinct, or where, I don't know, Hitler was just an artist?" She felt herself carried by a peculiar momentum: the Pit, the cosmic trash heap, the dumping ground for debris from infinity, the rip in the fabric of the multiverse; the precarious, hazardous seam. "Or the world where the three of us are religious zealots rather than paleobotanists, or maybe just the world where once I put strawberry jam on my sandwich in seventh grade rather than apricot jam. What if stuff from all those places slips through the Pit into our—"

She stopped, noticing how intently Roz and Corey were gazing at her.

"Yeah," Roz said. "I get what you mean."

Corey sighed grandly. "Hey, I love sci-fi as much as the next dork."

"It's not science fiction," Roz countered.

Molly looked at her. Had Roz, too, met her double, another Roz?

Her milk came down.

"It's a metaphor," Roz continued. "That's what fossils from dead lineages are, you know? Messengers from alternate realities. Fifi is just one possible future that didn't pan out. I think of it that way too. So, is the Bible on the premises?"

"I don't know where it is." *Not a metaphor,* Molly wanted to say, feeling extraordinarily lonely, *not a—*

But she need not be lonely. There was someone.

One person who understood everything, and more.

"Just bring the Bible and the other artifacts back tomorrow," Roz said.

"I can keep them at bay for one day," Corey said, "maybe."

"After all, we have to make a living, right?" Roz said.

"Living-ish," Corey quipped on his way out.

15

It was a warm, raw day. Standing in front of the Phillips 66 she saw many shades of gray and white (the field, the sky, the highway entrance ramp). She had stepped out for fresh air, to clear her head, to try to make some kind of plan, but when she opened the door all the people on Corey's Tuesday-morning tour turned to look at her, and kept looking over at her amid their questions as to the current whereabouts of the Bible, and she went back inside after less than a minute.

She was sweating, sweating an excessive amount, and her bra was damp; her self-created wetnesses were increasing her anxiety.

Who had taken the Bible?

She went to the bank of lockers in the windowless employee room in the back—a holdover from the gas station days—where she and Corey and Roz kept spare clothes for when they got too dirty in the Pit. She couldn't remember the last time she had opened her locker but she was pretty sure there was a spare shirt in there.

When she opened it, a clot of clothing fell onto her feet.

She leaped back.

A clot of blood-encrusted clothing.

She could smell it. The rust.

Jeans, a black shirt.

That stiffness of the jeans.

The same black shirt she happened to be wearing today.

16

Molly was pulling out of the parking lot of the Phillips 66 when the black car pulled into the parking lot: a clean, compact vehicle with that rental-car gleam.

She reached for her bag, on the passenger seat beside her, shoving past the bloody clothing in search of her phone. She dialed Corey with her thumb as she drove along the frontage road. She could pull a U-turn—she could, she should.

But the extent of her bravery was to call Corey.

"Wait did you leave?" Corey said. "Roz was just—"

"Is there a woman in a black car in the parking lot?"

"I'm in my office."

"Can you go and check?"

"Sure."

She waited.

"Corey?"

"Just a sec. I just have to send this email."

"Please, quick, check, right now. But stay inside. Don't go outside. Okay?"

"Molly! Okay, okay, okay. Okay, I'm walking to the front. Okay, I'm looking at the parking lot."

"And?"

"Yep. Black car. About to park."

"Is she wearing a sweatshirt?"

"Wait, never mind. Not parking. Just passing through."

Just passing through.

"Is she wearing a sweatshirt?"

"I'm not even sure she's a she. But anyway it's leaving now."

Molly did pull a U-turn then, but by the time she was back in front of the Phillips 66 parking lot, there was no black car in sight.

She pulled a second U-turn. She was making herself dizzy.

She opened all the windows in the hope that the wind would clear her head, but it just increased the dizziness. She closed the windows. But that was too airless. She opened them again.

Stopped at a red light, she watched a woman with a baby in a carrier in the crosswalk. The woman was missing both forearms. Molly was filled with pity (How would you bathe it, nurse it, put it to bed?) until the angle changed and she realized the missing forearms had been a trick of her eyes.

She kept waiting for the bloody clothing to shimmer or disappear or otherwise start to seem less real than the corresponding clothing she was wearing.

But it remained there on the passenger seat, spilling out of her bag, unchanging, inactive: real.

That blood was the blood of her children.

That's what it was.

She could take it to a lab, get it tested, find out if the DNA matched.

She made a left where she should have made a right, drove toward the reservoir. The day was still gray and white. There was green in places, blue in places, but what she saw was the gray and the white. She parked in the turnabout beside the bridge and cradled the clothing as she walked to the middle of the bridge, acutely aware of the two wet patches of milk on her chest.

She hesitated only an instant before hurling the clothes into the water. The cars and trucks rushed behind her, loud and divinely indifferent.

She thought she would feel relieved but she did not feel relieved.

There was one other pedestrian on the bridge, a gaunt man with a small camera. He stared at her. Then he pointed his camera straight up and took a picture of the sky.

17

The children were cranky. Maybe everyone would be better off if Erika had stayed until the appointed time. If Molly, after parting with the clothes, had continued to drive dizzy around the gray and white world with the wind in the car.

But at least today she had not been usurped by Moll.

She couldn't stand her phone, the long record of missed calls and declined video chats and neglected texts from David. She couldn't stand the cluttered surface of her home desk, all the unopened mail, couldn't stand to glance at her email, the untended in-box overgrown with notifications from Viv's school and pleas from good causes and notes from various people she knew. How exotic, outrageous, the normal business of life.

As soon as one child stopped whining, the other child would begin whining. And then, sometimes, a duet.

She needed to make a plan, some way to navigate these hours, to distract the children enough that she could let her thoughts run along their own fretful tracks.

The plan was: *Let's go and sit on the front steps and count the passing cars.* Like watching paint dry. Okay, but a plan is a plan. A plan is power, anticipation, kids jumping up and down, clapping their hands, no matter how feeble the plan.

"We're going to the steps! To count cars!" Viv shepherded Ben to the front door.

"Bebock," Ben said.

"What?" Molly said.

"Bebock," he said.

"Come on," Molly said, rushing them though there was no rush. Just the rush to escort them into a few minutes of peace.

They were both, finally, out the door. She pulled it shut behind them, wanting to draw a solid line between the place where they had been cranky and the place where they would no longer be cranky.

The door would not close. She yanked harder. There was resistance, something preventing it from shutting the final half centimeter, maybe a strong draft blowing through the house? Maybe a toy jammed on the other side of the hinges? Maybe someone pulling on the door with equal force from the opposite side?

Or, she realized only as Ben's howl took root in his bowels and rose upward: Ben's right ring finger, somehow lodged in just the wrong place, the place that she had been clamping with all her force.

In horror she reopened the door, releasing the finger, and both she and Viv descended upon him in a fruitless effort to comfort. For a long time the three of them were suspended in a moment from which there was no escape: the shrieking boy, the terrified sister, the guilty mother.

The finger seemed fine.

Or so she told herself. He wouldn't let her get a good look at it.

After a while, the sound of bagpipes could be heard a long way off.

"What's that?" Viv said, lifting her head from the spot where she had nuzzled into Molly's shoulder.

"Bagpipes," Molly explained to Viv over the noise of Ben's weeping.

Slowly the bagpipes drew closer. Ben stopped crying. He listened.

"He should have said 'Excuse me' to the door. Right, Mom? If he had said 'Excuse me' to the door this wouldn't have happened."

Ben crawled into Molly's lap and stood on her legs and wrapped his arms around her neck and let her whisk the tears off his face. He tugged at her shirt. Her unmarred black shirt. She lifted it so he could nurse.

". . . up above the world so high, like a diamond in the sky . . . ," Viv sang along with the bagpipes.

It sounded weird, "Twinkle, Twinkle, Little Star" on the bagpipes.

Still nursing, Ben opened and closed his fingers for the twinkle part, as Viv had trained him to do. His right ring finger moving just as well as the others.

"Am I going to see the pagbipes?"

"Bagpipes. Yes. This is your first time ever seeing them I think." Yet another item on the near-infinite list of things to which she had introduced Viv.

"And then her mother took her to the ruined schoo-oo-ool!" Viv sang along with the next verse.

"What?"

"And then her mother took her to the ruined schoo-oo-ool!" Viv continued.

"Who told you those words?"

"Made them up."

The sound of the bagpipes came ever nearer. The musician turned the corner. A young woman. She was not playing the bagpipes. She was playing a reed instrument that Molly didn't recognize.

"Bagpipes!" Viv said.

18

Viv wanted to go into Ben's crib with him so they could pretend to be newborns. As Molly lifted them in (thinking that she was not doing a very good job, that in a mere twenty minutes she had wounded the baby and misinformed the child), her foot came into contact with something bulky beneath the crib.

Her big old brown duffel bag, shoved into the shadows, packed so full its contents strained the zipper.

"Why's the suitcase under here?" Molly said. "What's in it?"

Viv looked at her strangely.

"Everything we put in it, of course," she said.

"Toys?"

"Mom, you know."

Molly reached for it.

"Leave us alone!" Viv said. "Close the door!"

Molly dragged the duffel out to the living room. She unzipped it: a good bit of the kids' clothing, some of their favorite stuffed animals and blankets.

She found her phone. She called David. It was time.

But his phone went straight to voice mail.

She called him again, staring at the duffel. She had the urge to scream, to leave such a scream on his voice mail that he would come to them at once; that even if they were gone when he arrived, he would know to search for them, would know to assume the worst.

But instead she left a message: asked him to call her as soon as possible, put enough of an edge in her voice that he would understand she meant it. He would recognize that she was ready, now, to explain why she had been the way she had been.

After hanging up, she was struck by the silence coming from the children's room.

The scream lingered just inside her, searing, awaiting its moment.

She gathered herself before opening their bedroom door.

19

Moll was not in the basement.

Molly said her name once, twice.

So where was she? Out in the world? With the Bible and the other artifacts? Enacting some plan? Laying the groundwork for a kidnapping?

Then, she spotted Moll beyond a stack of cardboard boxes, on the folding chair at the base of the window well, staring upward at the slight light, holding the metal pipe upright in her left hand like a cane.

It was the chair where Molly sat when she came down late at night to listen to him play. Once in a while she could see the moon from there, bright at the top of the window well. It gave her an odd sense of familiarity, to see Moll there, to witness herself perched on her perch.

"Please," Moll said. "Go away."

The cold voice of someone looking back on two pregnancies, two births, all the months of breastfeeding, the years of exhaustion and bliss? The cold voice of someone considering the androgyny of the skeletons of children?

"Why did you pack the duffel?" Molly said.

Moll cleared her throat, a painful sound.

"You," Moll said, "always have to check to make sure their fingers aren't in the door."

Molly's first instinct was to defend herself, she was only human, but when instead she agreed, "I should have been more careful," the self-flagellation came as a relief.

"I should have been more careful," Moll repeated.

She had yet to look at Molly. She was only looking upward, outward, into the window well. Molly watched her every movement, kept her eyes on the metal pipe that could at any second become a weapon. But Moll hardly moved.

"We were playing," Moll said. "Vacation."

It was then that Molly registered the five-by-seven white rectangle placed directly, deliberately, beneath the folding chair. Though the photograph was facing downward, Molly knew what it was: the single image David kept in the basement, taped above his keyboard, a picture he had taken last Halloween of Molly holding Viv and Ben (a spider, a ladybug) on the front steps. She recalled their resistance, their glee, their bodies straining away from her.

A photograph, she realized, is a fossil.

"You can do dinner," Molly said. Astonished, as she said it, by her exceptional generosity, momentarily forgetting that it was a generosity tinged with fear. She took off her black shirt and

263

unzipped her jeans and awaited Moll's happiness. That permanent raw greediness in her eyes abating somewhat in the moments before she was reunited with them.

But still Moll did not look at her, standing there in bra and underwear in the chill of her cellar.

Molly held her shed clothes out to Moll.

Moll wouldn't touch them.

Only then did Molly (stupid) remember what these clothes were.

"They both fell asleep in his crib," Molly said to ward off the silence.

"Okay," Moll said wearily. "I'll go up."

20

It was silent upstairs. Molly pictured Moll standing in the kitchen, not moving a muscle. Standing in the living room, not moving a muscle. Wearing sweatpants and a stained T-shirt so she wouldn't have to wear the clothing she was wearing when.

Then the children broke the silence and Moll's footsteps hurried to their bedroom. Molly listened to their varied tones: excited to insistent to tender to pleading to agreeable, the many emotions passing in and out of her children's voices, all of them met by Moll's equanimity.

Molly searched for the baby monitor, found it under the futon, listened to her own voice speaking to her own children with love. She turned the monitor off and tossed it back under the futon.

She both wanted and didn't want to creep up the basement steps into the bush.

From inside the evergreen, she could see Viv and Ben stacking blocks on the living room floor while Moll made dinner in the kitchen.

That perfect peace of children playing when

they know their mother is nearby. Knowing she is there, they can ignore her completely.

When Moll called the children to the table, both were alarmingly compliant, going right over and submitting themselves to their respective seats.

Moll had prepared a plate for herself too, had gotten herself a glass of water, and sat down across from them.

Molly, when David was out of town, never sat with the kids to eat; while they had dinner, she rushed around getting a head start on the end-of-day cleanup.

"There's a big party going on inside our bodies," Viv said.

Viv's voice was far louder than Moll's; Molly couldn't hear Moll's response.

"A party of blood and bones and our brain and stuff," Viv clarified.

Again Molly couldn't hear Moll's response. But she could see that Moll was smiling.

Molly exited the bush. Instead of returning to the basement she walked around the house to the sidewalk.

She felt reckless, uncareful. March was about to give way to April and she could feel it in the air, a certain levity. The dusk was gray but there was a glimmer at its edges, a silver indication in the clouds. The neighborhood starting to smell more like plants, less like car exhaust.

She never took walks by herself at dusk. This

was the time of day when her home demanded everything of her. Once in a while she would peek out the window at the tail end of a sunset. But always she was needed inside.

Now, though, having achieved her wish, walking these streets alone at the sunset hour, she felt unmoored, the appalling vertigo of her freedom.

She walked. The glimmer spread across the sky, black birds writing cursive on it with their bodies.

21

Moll was lying on the rug in the living room with her eyes closed. Viv and Ben were circling around her, poking at her with instruments from their toy doctor kit.

Molly watched from the evergreen, straining to catch every gesture: Ben smacking Moll's knee with the thermometer, Viv struggling to fit the child-size blood pressure cuff around Moll's upper arm.

Frustrated, Viv threw the blood pressure cuff to the side and grabbed the thermometer out of Ben's hand. Ben shrieked and stumbled over Moll's body in his effort to reclaim the thermometer. But Moll did not stir, did not use her arms to brace his fall. His cheek hit the floor and he began to cry.

Still Moll did not move. Viv tried to wrench Moll's mouth open in order to shove the thermometer in. Ben, ignored by both of them, stopped wailing and began whimpering. He crawled to the doctor kit and pulled out the stethoscope. When Viv saw that he had the stethoscope, she ran over and snatched it away, relaunching his crying fit.

Moll remained immobile, unspeaking, on the floor.

Was she asleep?

But she was not. Her face (Molly craned, craned harder, to spy through the window at the necessary angle) was tight, tense, not the face of a sleeper.

"Mommy!" the children yelled as they pulled on opposite ends of the stethoscope, waiting for her to intervene with some just plan. "Mommy! Mommy!"

When Moll failed to respond, they looked over at her. Their shared chant took on a tenor of doubt: "Mommy? Mommy? Mommy?"

Viv flung herself on the prone body, and then Ben did too, Viv ferociously patting Moll's face, Ben tugging on her hair and fingers.

Moll did not react.

The children scooted back a bit, stared at her.

"Are you alive?" Viv shouted at Moll's body, beginning to cry.

Molly had to go in. Never mind that they shouldn't see two mothers at once. Their caretaker was toxic with grief. It was insane that she had ever let Moll be with them.

She was at the back door, about to stride through it, when Moll opened her eyes.

"Oh Mama," Viv said. Her voice sounded like the voice of a much older person.

Ben threw himself over Moll, matching his

torso to her torso, his arms and legs miniature versions atop hers. That well-known weight of him.

Viv sat cross-legged at the crown of Moll's head, prying Moll's head off the floor and into her lap. Moll should have resisted (it was ridiculous, a grown woman with her head in a little girl's lap), but she did not resist, she put her head in Viv's lap, and Viv stroked her face.

22

Molly in the cellar, listening on the baby monitor, knew when Moll went in to nurse Ben in the rocking chair (the milk itching in her own echoing breasts); knew when she stood to place him in the crib; knew when Viv ran to the bookshelf to choose a book.

Moll had gathered herself. Was managing to do everything just so.

Once she was certain that Moll was ensconced in the children's room, getting Viv to sleep and probably, in the process, accidentally falling asleep herself, Molly exited the basement and entered through the back door.

She sat on the couch, preparing her words, gathering her bravery and her cruelty.

You have to admit.

This is not.

This cannot.

You are a danger to them.

It was a long time before Moll came down the hallway, unsteady. Molly knew that feeling, felt it in herself as she witnessed it in Moll, the effort of pulling oneself out of sleep after those involuntary bedtime naps. The slight nausea, the bloodshot eyes.

Moll, foggy, did not notice Molly. She stood in the entry to the kitchen, leaning against the wall, devastated, surveying the detritus of dinner, the dishes and the crumbs, but Moll's devastation was universes away from Molly's nightly despair of resurfacing from the children's bedroom into the disorder of the house, that mundane fleeting luxurious despair.

Watching Moll staring at the mess (staring at it, not seeing it), Molly found her severity softening, losing its shape. She tried to keep it firm, its hard edges intact.

But Moll's face was the color of grief.

"I can help," Molly said eventually.

She had struggled to land on those three words. She had considered so many others. *You have to. You are a.*

When Moll glanced over at her, Molly realized that she had in fact already registered her presence. Was not surprised by her voice.

You are a, Molly wanted to say, *you are a,* but found herself unable.

You could go back, or try to, she thought to say.

But go back how? Who knew what rules governed the Pit, the seam?

And to what? To whom?

She thought of the other David, the bereaved one. She saw his face with sudden, terrible clarity.

Molly got up off the couch and walked over to Moll, who scooted into the kitchen, perhaps to make room for Molly in the space, though it seemed more like someone straining out of the reach of flames.

Molly opened the cabinet under the sink and got the orange-clove spray and misted the counter-tops. The spray bottle sputtered, almost empty.

"We're running out," Molly said, to combat the void, Moll's epic silence. It took her a second to notice that she had said *we.* She could pretend she had intended the *we* to refer to herself and David. But she knew whom she had meant by *we.* They cleaned together in the known order, listening to the sound—or the nonsound—of the children's sleep. A curious camaraderie with the person she wanted to eliminate, the person who wanted to eliminate her.

"What's this?" Molly said, reaching under the table to pick up a piece of paper. It bore a series of letters in Viv's oversize handwriting: *ILVBTULVMIEXEBX.*

" 'I love you because you love my coloring book,' " Moll translated.

Amused, Molly looked at Moll, but she kept her head down, sweeping the floor.

"Bebock," Moll said, "means *peacock.* When he says *peacock,* he means *pigeon."*

And Molly thought, a passing flash: *Maybe. Maybe we could—*

"Mommy," Viv sang out from the bedroom. "I'm not asleep anymore."

Molly stiffened, awaited Moll's request. Her begging eyes.

But Moll had already given up, had already put down the broom, was already heading toward the back door, her shoulders wilting with fatigue.

23

"I have to pee," Viv said, emerging from the bedroom just as Moll vanished.

She looked skinny and sleepy, her curly hair dark and huge around her small face.

Molly fell toward her, grabbed her and held her.

"Mom," Viv said, "I said I have to pee."

Molly smelled her hair, her eyebrows.

"Excuse me," Viv said. "Mom!"

"Okay fine go."

After Viv had mounted the toilet, she requested a coloring book.

"No way," Molly said. "You're going right back to bed."

Viv sighed.

"Ready to get off or are you still peeing?"

"Still peeing," Viv lied.

Molly decided to let her sit for another couple of minutes while she completed Moll's interrupted sweeping task.

"The bugs are coming!" Viv cried out.

Molly ran back into the bathroom. It was illuminated only by the glow of a night-light.

"Where?" Molly said.

"What?" Viv said.

"The bugs."

"What bugs?"

"You screamed 'The bugs are coming!' "

Viv laughed. "I did?"

Perplexed, Molly handed her three squares of toilet paper.

"Can you stay with me the whole night?" Viv said.

"You don't sleep as well if I'm in your bed."

"But I'm so scared tonight."

"Why?" Viv's fear refreshed Molly's anxiety, made it newly raw and pressing.

"I don't feel safe."

"Why not?" A child's sixth sense that something was unsteady in the household—that her mother was not always her mother?

"Please, just stay with me the whole night."

"Well," Molly said, trying to ignore the agitation rising in her, "maybe."

"Yay." Viv hopped off the toilet and grabbed Molly's hand.

It had always seemed a bit deceitful to Molly, the way we put our children to bed in soft pajamas, give them milk, read them books, locate their stuffed creatures, tell them that all is well, there's nothing to be scared of, as though sleep isn't one-sixteenth of death. When they resist the prospect of sleep, of long dark lonely hours, intuiting that this is indeed a rehearsal for death, we murmur to them, we rub their backs, pretending they will never die. Little do they know that behind our backs we keep our fingers crossed, and that our hearts too thump with anguish when we turn off our bedside lamps.

She rubbed circles around Viv's back with the palm of her hand.

"Don't worry." Sleep is not a sip of death. "Don't worry." I am here and I always will be. "Don't worry."

24

In the process of sedating Viv, she sedated herself too. She fell into a sort of drowse, and when she finally managed to extricate herself from it, she found that her anxiety had slipped away. A dark, solemn peace filled her. The house was clean, the children sacrificed to sleep.

But then, going down the hallway back toward the living room, she heard something.

The *kaboom, kaboom, kaboom* of a beating heart.

She tried to be logical. Maybe her phone had somehow started playing one of David's tracks that included this sound effect. Maybe a nearby car was blasting music with this exact drumbeat. Maybe the neighbors were watching a horror movie.

But what it sounded like, what it really sounded like, was a heart beating right in her living room.

And what she knew, what she fully knew, was that Moll was responsible for it.

The sound, she realized, originated from the couch.

She did not want to approach the couch, did not

want to find whatever she would find beneath the cushion from which (she was now nearly certain) the sound emanated.

A huntsman ripping a heart out of a girl or a deer, carrying it back to the evil queen in a wooden box. She half covered her eyes with one hand and yanked the cushion off the couch with the other.

The heartbeat stopped.

The children's stethoscope. The cushion had been compressing the red heartbeat button.

She laughed, alone, the hardest she had ever laughed alone in her life.

Once she had recovered, still giddy, she thought of Moll, below her in the cellar. Pacing, perhaps, or perhaps sitting, or perhaps somber in sleep. She would go to Moll. She would tell her about the heartbeat.

Then she would insist that Moll run upstairs to sleep in the big bed. Would urge her to carry the children from their room into hers. Go up, she would say. Go sleep in the grass of their sleep.

25

Her heart was shockingly light as she stepped barefoot across the dark yard. Here she was, about to do the right thing. It occurred to her to surprise Moll, to give her this gift with that extra flourish, so she lifted the heavy doors as deftly as possible.

The cellar was unlit, but there were sounds coming from it.

Could she blame Moll, though? Hadn't it crossed her mind more than once, during those desolate basement hours, to do the same, surrounded by his instruments and the smells of him? To use it as a brief but absolute escape. A momentary entry into an alternate mode of being.

The sound of Moll's—of her own—hungry breathing.

She took another step down the staircase, creating a creak, but the breathing continued, ignorant or indifferent. Should she advance or retreat?

She stepped down, and down again, but her movements had no effect on the breathing, the swelling orchestra of breathing coming from the futon.

Her eyes adjusted. The red light of the numbers on the digital clock illuminated the futon.

There were two bodies.

Two familiar bodies.

She was on top, leaning over him so their foreheads touched. Then tilting her head so her teeth met his teeth, that vicious way they sometimes liked to kiss.

She could not fully see the kiss—what she saw was her butt moving up and down, up and down, up and down—but she knew exactly what kind of kiss it was.

She despised her body for its response to the scene. For the way it bore disorientation and envy and rage and desire all at once.

She couldn't look away: she had to watch it, this righteous, joyous fucking. She recognized it as the sort where you fall back down afterward and laugh together, smug, because now you've got something on the whole rest of the world.

His hands grabbed her waist and pulled it down hard to still its movement so he would not come. Inside the cock pulsed: one, two, three times. She felt it. The tenderness of the hands on the hips.

He stretched his neck up off the mattress to take her nipple between his teeth. He flicked it with his tongue.

It was rare, so rare, now, with the kids, that they

281

got to be together this way, but they had, so many times, in their life together, been together this way, and it had been, still was, when it happened, such a good thing. She was hurting, watching. She knew what he was about to do and then he did it: flipped her over so she was beneath him. Trailed his lips down her body, between her breasts, past her belly button, the place where they had grown, the place where they had come out. The place where now she needed his mouth.

From this position, Moll could see Molly. Their eyes met as he began. Molly imagined it on her own body, the uncontainable pleasure, but there was no pleasure in Moll's eyes: only grief.

26

Molly lurched back up the steps, across the grass, through the screen door. Only once she was inside did she realize she had neglected to close the cellar doors. But she would not go back out there.

She had sipped of the lust and now she drank of the grief.

She staggered to the couch and lost her children, and lost them, and lost them, and lost them.

— PART 5 —

1

She was standing at the sink, washing grapes for the kids' breakfast, when a hand touched her waist, setting off a startled shiver that vibrated through her body.

But he kept his hand there, and his touch contained everything: the sex from last night, the gratitude for her days alone with the kids, the years and years behind them and ahead of them. Under other circumstances, she would have been so happy.

The last time she had seen him, four hours ago, at three in the morning, she had crept down the cellar stairs to find him asleep on the futon, naked, embracing a pillow with his arms and legs as though it were her, the baby monitor right by his ear and turned up to its highest volume, his unopened suitcase beside the futon, his travel instruments sealed in their cases, awaiting their return to their pedestals.

She had stood over him, worrying about Moll, for there was no sign of Moll.

Molly went back up the stairs but she couldn't sleep. She had not even tried to sleep in her own bed. She had tried to sleep in Viv's bed, but it was too cramped for an insomniac.

Moll was gone. The metal pipe was gone.

"You're all alive and well," David observed as she continued to rinse the grapes. She didn't look at him but she could hear his smile, its old wryness, and his relief that her distraction had not been indicative of any grave crisis. "I was beginning to wonder."

Her mind was empty, incapable of coming up with any response. She imagined Moll feeling the same way last night, stunned at his unexpected arrival. How she might have, probably did, swerve the situation into sex so as to avoid conversation.

"It's been busy," she said.

"I'm sure it has," he said; beneath the four agreeable words lay his reproach for her stand-offishness while he was away.

She separated the grapes that were too soft from the grapes that were firm, still unable to reassure him. She was thinking about Moll.

"I thought you were getting home on Saturday," she said. "It's only Wednesday."

"Sacramento," he said, "remember?"

"Sacramento?"

"I knew you weren't paying attention."

She said nothing. She focused on the grapes. He waited.

"My flight leaves at two this afternoon," he said.

"Okay," she said, grateful for the noncommittal word.

"They're paying double because of the change."

"Okay." She didn't want to tell him anything that would unsettle this reality, this well-known reality of them together in the kitchen, soon to be interrupted by the ones they loved above all else.

"I can walk Viv to school and be with Ben till I have to go. I'll text Erika."

"Okay."

He reached around her and turned off the faucet. He said her name twice. He held her. It was good to be held by him. She rested, briefly, against him. It had always been rich between them, it had been hard at times and they had had their times of anger, but it had always been rich and true, and she did not know how to talk to him when she was not being true, when she could not speak truly.

"Daddy?" A quartet of sticky feet coming down the hall. "Daddy?"

2

Corey was looking at her funny, and she realized he had asked her the same question multiple times.

And then the question registered, then it hit her: "Did you go home to shower?"

She responded with a head gesture that could be read either way.

"I saw you out there when I got here," he said. "Car in the shop? Went to the Pit to say hi after putting coffee on but you were gone."

"You saw me? What was I wearing?"

"I don't know, Molly. Pants and a shirt! Find anything?"

"What was I doing?"

"I don't know. What were you doing?"

"What do you think I was doing?"

"A little early-morning precrowd excavation—right? Because you heard that Roz found another Fifi Flower specimen yesterday and you want to find one too?"

"But where was I exactly?" Molly persisted, barely hearing him.

"Molly."

"You could see me. So I wasn't in the Pit. I was near the Pit. But do you think I was going down or coming up?"

"Molly!" Corey laughed. "Seriously, though, we're waiting on you. The Bible?"

"I feel like shit," she said. The words fell so far short of the feeling.

"Yeah you've been kind of a mess this week. Why don't you leave the Bible and friends with me and go home, rest up."

"Okay," Molly said, inching toward the doorway, past Corey, "I—"

And she exited her cubicle, and hurried down the hallway, and out the glass door, ignoring Corey's voice repeating her name.

She wanted to run straight to her car, but she knew that first she had to force herself to go and look into the Pit.

This was the only reason she had come to work: to search for Moll.

What she saw when she envisioned the Pit was Moll, facedown, star-shaped in the mud.

She began the thirty-yard journey hesitantly, dreading the downward glance, the potential corpse, but by the end she was sprinting to reach the edge of the Pit.

3

As Molly pulled out of the parking lot—already filling up with vehicles in anticipation of the morning tour—she waved to Corey, who must have had his eye on her from the doorway. She saw him in her rearview mirror, standing in the open door, saying something in her direction. He was suspicious, so suspicious and so kind. She turned the proper direction out of the parking lot to make him believe that she was going home to rest up and return to herself.

Roz was arriving in her truck just as Molly was leaving in her car. Roz eyed her, let go of the steering wheel to gesture an aggressive question with her hands and elbows, and though Molly was vaguely moved by Roz's understandable exasperation, she just waved and accelerated.

The Pit had looked like a pit, nothing more, no portal, no seam, no body, no locus of cosmic arrivals and departures: just mud and puddles. The soft rubble of dirt moistened and dried and moistened and dried and moistened again. There were footprints encircling the Pit, footprints leading down into it. She knelt to examine them. They matched the soles of the sneakers on her feet. She had lost her balance for an instant, had felt herself sliding down the side, laden with small bodies.

She passed through an intersection, another intersection, another intersection.

Only then did Corey's question strike her: *Car in the shop?* Meaning—what? That he had seen in the parking lot, when he saw Moll at the Pit, some unknown car?

So where was Moll?

Could Molly imagine her way through the blast, the loss, the seam, the grief, the rage, the plan, the days, the sex, the flight, in order to determine the location of her other? The person who was perhaps in hiding, plotting her next and darkest step. The person who was perhaps in dire need of help and comfort, food and shelter.

Where would she herself go under those circumstances?

What would she herself be capable of?

But she did not know herself well enough to answer the first question, and she did not dare to answer the second.

She drove around, speculating. She drove to the reservoir. The wind blowing, the sky colorless. It alarmed her how little it bothered her, the fact of Moll and David's sex. How natural, almost obvious, it seemed: David had slept with his wife, Moll had slept with her husband.

When her milk came down, she thought of Moll's coming down too. It was the first time her milk had come down today. Now that he was getting half his milk from Moll, her supply was diminishing.

She imagined saying to Moll, *What happens if you're trying to pump while also having any kind of disagreement, small or large, with David?*

No milk, Moll would reply.

Weird, right?

Remember that first shit after giving birth? Moll would volley back.

Scary, right?

And with each exchange, Molly's body would grow more excited, an inner flush spreading through her at the affirmation of their shared random memories, a shedding of all loneliness, a level of unity rapidly approaching the divine. She dreamed of asking Moll never-ending questions, dreamed of hearing Moll's *Yes. Yes. Yes.*

She drove around, desperate. The urgency of her search was undeniable: she felt it in each part of her body, everything pounding, elevated, dizzy. But she could not tell whether it was the urgency of tracking down an enemy or the urgency of looking for a friend. She was terrified of Moll. She was worried about Moll.

There was a particular bench she liked. There was a particular café. Everywhere she went she felt as though Moll had just been there. Yet she couldn't bring herself to ask anyone, "Excuse me, have you by chance seen a woman identical to me but wearing dirty sweatpants?"

She sat in the parked car in the uncomfortable heat, immobilized by the what-ifs, the swiftness with which anything can change, the ever-present split second that is the difference between blood spilling or not, the difference between one future and another. She contemplated equally the possibility that Moll had slipped away for all eternity and the possibility that Moll would reappear at any moment to kill her.

Where was she?

Molly was unlocking the door to Norma's house when she remembered that Norma was back from her trip. She did not want to see Norma. She did not want to see anybody. Only one person. But here came Norma, through the kitchen with her walker.

"Forget something?" Norma said.

So Moll had indeed done the same: had gone to Norma's, had unlocked the door before realizing the house was no longer uninhabited.

Molly stepped inside. The kitchen still buzzed from her first encounter with Moll. It was the same as ever: the tarnished copper kettle, the red-and-white-checkered fabric, the strawberry lamp. Yet now it buzzed with something, and would forevermore.

"It really will take me a while to get over your

slaughter of my plants," Norma said. "But still, do you want another cup of tea?"

Norma was tall and keen and now, often, ill. The word *BLOOD* on the whiteboard on the fridge had been replaced by the word *PAY,* in the same blue letters.

"How was Arizona?" Molly said, trying to think of what one ought to say.

"I thought I was supposed to be the one in danger of senility," Norma shot back.

"I should—" Molly said, struggling to facilitate a graceful exit. Feeling guilty, rude. "—the kids."

Norma was, as ever, unruffled. "Yes, I thought you were in a rush to get back to them. Go! Go! Don't forget to tell them I got them a dodo."

Driving home she thought of the night—she refused to believe it was only five nights ago—when Moll, silent and unknown, had driven her to Norma's house. The way the car had smelled of papier-mâché.

Through the side window Molly spied Erika giving the children a snack at the table. She snuck across the yard, went to the basement to look for Moll.

Standing at the bottom of the steps, Molly took note of the cardboard box (now shoved partway under the futon) that Moll had brought down two nights ago, the box containing their most mundane favorites, the scarf, the hoodie, the T-shirt, the socks. At the time she had believed it was a threat, a sign of Moll settling in, taking possession of all her precious things. Only now did it occur to her that Moll had brought it down so both of them could be a little more comfortable during their long cellar hours, could have a hint of solace.

She checked every corner, every shadow, but Moll was not in the basement.

4

Upstairs, the kids were out of sorts, and Erika was out of sorts too. Erika was never out of sorts. She took the cash from Molly and hurried off, gathering herself just enough to mutter, "Sorry, I'm so not feeling great."

Viv kept begging for things (a video, a Popsicle), and, weak, Molly acquiesced.

Ben didn't want to do anything except nurse. Even once he had drained both breasts still he wanted to suckle. She let him, held him, but after a while it became ridiculous and she had to get dinner on the table. She pulled him off her and set him on the rug, surrounded by toys. He howled as though she had orphaned him.

Where was Moll?

She finally put her foot down vis-à-vis the videos and instructed Viv to entertain her brother. Viv built a block tower. Ben knocked it over. Viv screamed at him. Ben tried and failed to throw a block at his sister.

"Relax!" Molly found herself shrieking. "Relax!"

Neither child would eat a bite of the dinner she had prepared. No pasta? No carrot? No banana? No graham cracker with peanut butter?

No! No! No! No! No!

Come to think of it, the food was repulsive to her too.

Bath time, early bedtime. She could make it. Somehow she would make it.

Oh, but Viv did not want to take a bath. She could remember the last time she had taken a bath and she did not like to take a new bath until she had forgotten her old bath.

Ben calmed down a notch or two in the warm water. Molly took refuge in the honeysuckle scent of the baby wash. She realized how acutely part of her was waiting, ever alert to the possibility of Moll's footsteps in the other room.

Viv ran up and down the hall, chanting. Only after a few minutes did the words of Viv's chant register with Molly:

"In my scary dream, I saw the mystery! In my scary dream, I saw the mystery!"

"Viv," Molly called. "What's that you're saying?"

"A song." Viv skipped into the bathroom, grabbed one of Ben's bath cups, scooped up water, and tossed it at his face. He cried.

"Viv!" Molly roared.

"I was cleaning him," Viv claimed, skipping away. "In my scary dream, I saw the mystery!"

"Where did you hear that song?" Molly yelled down the hallway.

"In my scary dream! I saw the mystery!"

"Vivian, where did you hear that song?"

"In my head," Viv chirped.

Molly wanted to probe further—what the fuck?—but Ben was upset, wet from bathwater and wet from tears, a bedraggled little otter, so she pulled him dripping out of the bath, onto her lap, forgetting to place a towel there first.

"I'm doing a good job rhyming, right?" Viv poked her head into the bathroom.

Ben threw up on Molly's shoulder, a spew of half-chewed raisins and breast milk.

She twisted him around and he threw up again, this time on her knees and on the bath mat and on Viv's toes.

5

"Turn on the light! Turn on the light!"

It was—what?—the middle of the night.

Who was talking to her? Was Ben talking to her? Ben was not talking to her. Ben could not talk. Ben was sleeping beside her in the big bed because she once heard of a baby who choked to death on its own vomit. Ben's skin was hot, too hot, to the touch. And in the dark someone kept telling her to turn on the light. And that person was becoming more upset by the second.

She couldn't find the switch for the bedside lamp.

She found the switch for the bedside lamp.

Viv was standing beside the bed.

"I'm bad," Viv said.

"You're bad?"

"I feel bad."

"Bad how?"

"Can you cover that mirror?" Viv was staring at the mirrored closet.

"Cover the mirror?"

"Please," Viv implored.

"Why?" It was a big mirror. She had no idea how she would go about covering it.

"I'm scared to see myself in the mirror."

"Why?" She reached for Viv's hand. Too hot to the touch.

Viv threw up on the pillow, on the sheets, on the rug, on Molly.

6

Her body woke her before daylight with a single pressing need.

She understood that her nausea was residual, merely a form of empathy for the two small humans who now slept (parched, fitful) beside her.

She had cleaned up so much last night—had lost count of the rounds—the children trading off—then overlapping—the only measure the laundry hamper reeking in the corner.

She leaned over them, breathed them in—their grassy aroma, her favorite smell in the world, obscured, now, by the stink of bile. The odor invaded her pores. The odor was to blame (she lay in bed, believing it) for this false response in her own stomach.

She hated throwing up. The beast within tearing through one's tamed body. Like giving birth. That same absolute loss of control.

Like orgasm too, but the opposite.

But this was no time for such thoughts.

Because she finally had to admit that the sourness was real, deep inside her—that she had to claim it, do something about it.

She extricated herself from the foul bed, the clammy children, and went to the bathroom and held the toilet.

Which was not as clean as one would have wished.

She considered fetching the toilet bowl cleaner from the cabinet, swooshing that blueness around the interior, sanitizing the victim of her embrace.

She discovered, though, that she had crossed the line: was past the point of being able to fetch and clean.

She crouched.

At first she hoped she wouldn't. Then she began to hope, fiercely, that she would. She just wanted to have the thing out of her. She just wanted to be free of it.

She waited.

It would not come.

She waited, an increasingly impatient passenger in a train station.

It did not come and it did not come and then, evil, it came.

7

In the bedroom, someone was throwing up.

She could not stand. She could not stand.

She stood. She walked to the bedroom.

Her foot slipped on a slick patch on the floor.

"I'm bad, I'm bad." Viv was weeping. "I just threw up on our baby."

Molly was too unsteady to speak but she sat on the bed and pulled Viv toward her. Ben slept on, splattered.

"Will he be okay?" Viv said.

Molly let go of Viv and ran back to the toilet. When she was done, she turned her head to see Viv in the doorway, freaking out.

"I'm okay," Molly lied. "Don't worry."

"He's awake now," Viv cried. "He's sick!"

There was no way she could handle this. It was impossible.

"Help me up," Molly said.

Viv looked at her and cried harder. But she did move closer to offer a useless little hand. Bolstered by the gesture alone, Molly somehow made it to her feet.

On the bed, Ben was crawling around in vomit

(apparently had just added to it himself), whimpering. She tried to pick him up but her arms were too wobbly. Instead, she sat them both on the edge of the bed and knelt down before them and laid her head half in his lap, half in her lap.

It was unclear whether this position indicated that she was reassuring them or that they were reassuring her. With extraordinary effort, she pulled her head up off their laps. They stared at her, their eyes moist.

Someone needed to do something.

She would call the doctor. That was something, a thing a person could do.

The pediatrician's twenty-four-hour hotline put her on hold. The children continued to stare at her. She held the slim phone with her shoulder and cupped the children's knees with her hands. After a while a young man told her, brightly, that she would receive a callback within forty-five minutes.

"Forty-five minutes?" She laughed. There was no way she would last that long.

"Erika?" Viv suggested as Molly hung up with a wrathful sob.

It was a brilliant idea. But Molly didn't pause to applaud Viv before texting Erika: *Can u come now? Emergency everyone throwing up.*

Only after pressing send did she note that the time was 6:03 a.m. So Erika would be deep asleep, childless, in the apartment she shared with several attractive roommates, dreaming of her upcoming backpacking trip, her alarm not set to go off for another hour and a half yet.

But an instant later Molly's phone buzzed with a text and she seized it.

Me 2! Erika replied. *Bad bug got us all, I'm destroyed, literally can't stand up, good luck lady! This sucks right*

So what now?

Norma, with her walker and her medications?

Those four scared and trusting eyes.

She called David. His phone went to voice mail. She called him six more times. Voice mail every time. Predawn Sacramento. She thought hateful thoughts about him.

She was still always about to throw up.

Moll, she thought with an odd flash of longing. And instantly corrected herself: Moll would be more dangerous than ever now, at this moment of utter vulnerability. If she were Moll, she acknowledged darkly, she would, yes, use this opportunity to—

The doctor called. It had been far less than forty-five minutes. She wept with gratitude.

The doctor was not concerned. The doctor said, "Don't give them any liquids for an hour after they vomit. Any liquid at all, including water, and they'll vomit again."

It was true that, all night long, worried about dehydration, she had given them sips of water

307

after they threw up, and, yes, they had kept throwing up.

"What about dehydration?" she said.

"Liquids are acceptable and essential, *after* an hour."

"What about breast milk?"

"*After* an hour."

"I'm sick too. I'm throwing up too."

"Oh," the doctor said.

Oh? she wanted to repeat back nastily, mocking the indifferent tone of this person who had taken the Hippocratic oath.

But instead she said, "Thank you."

Somehow the kids were in the bathtub. Somehow they had their bath toys. But the toys drifted, ignored, because what the children wanted was water to drink.

"Water, Mommy, please, water, please!" Viv entreated.

"Wawa," Ben joined in, "wawa, wawa," wailing.

"No," Molly kept saying like a wicked step-mother. "No water for you."

"Water, please! Just water!"

A woman denying her children water.

"Wawa, petah!" Rubbing his hand across his chest, the sign language for *please* that Erika had taught him, pleading with his words and his body, any way he knew how.

"I will," she said feebly, "set a timer. You have

to wait a while longer or you'll throw up again. That's what the doctor said. Do you want to throw up again?"

"I'm so thirsty, Mommy. It hurts, please."

Being a mother: it was too much.

"If you don't give me water then I'll drink the yucky bathwater," Viv threatened, changing tactics.

The bathwater was beyond yucky, a film of yellowish something on its surface.

"If you drink it you'll throw up again!" Molly rejoined, matching Viv's tone.

Viv's threats were paper-thin, and at the violence of her mother's response, she collapsed into tears. "Water, just water, please, please!"

"Fine!" Molly bellowed. "Fine, fine," unable to keep saying no. "Just a little."

She poured water into the metal cup by the sink. First Viv drank deep, then Ben. They smiled at her like she had given them chocolate milk.

Ill at the thought of Moll, ill in anticipation of what would soon emerge from them thanks to her weakness, she pulled up the toilet seat and vomited once more. They watched, appalled, from the bathtub.

8

The bed was a bog. The bog sucked downward on their three bodies, keeping them close, trapped. It would help if she changed the sheets. Perhaps if she changed the sheets the bog would go away. On clean sheets, they might have some chance of escape. Some chance of striking a defensive pose.

But there were no clean sheets. Last night she had changed the sheets again and again and now there were no more. She could not go to the basement to do laundry. She was not strong enough, not brave enough, to pull open those metal doors.

So these sheets, this bog.

And outside the window, a movement, a threat. A head, maybe, or a branch.

At least time had passed and now she could, every ten minutes or so, pull herself out of the haze to give each child a sip of water, which she poured into a teaspoon and ladled into the arid, stinking mouths.

She had tried, many times, to get Ben to nurse, wanting so much to give him something pure of hers, but he kept turning away as though revolted, and she felt her milk vanishing, drying up.

They passed in and out of sleep. When she was asleep she dreamed of them and when they were asleep they probably dreamed of her.

Only while they slept did she permit herself to believe that she would never make it out of this bed alive. That the next time they woke from nightmares she would be lying dead between them, and they would have to slide off the mattress by themselves and pull the fridge open and forage for food and drink water out of the bathtub faucet or the toilet until some adult heard them crying and came to take them away from her forever.

There was no one to take care of anyone.

She woke to the sensation of something on her skin, weird movements beneath her, the mattress sweaty and sentient; she didn't want to open her eyes but when at last she was bold enough to do so, she discovered that the bed was made of bodies, the naked bodies of sleeping women, women identical to Moll, identical to her, their bodies supporting her body, and she realized that she too was naked, indistinguishable from the rest, the heat of the others' skin partway pleasant, partway repulsive.

The movement on her skin was not the movement of bodies but rather the movement of Viv's fingers, tugging at her arm hairs.

"I want Mommy," Viv was saying, "I want Mommy," her voice rising.

The desire, the urgency and straightforwardness of it, yanked Molly into the moment. She was needed here; this she could do.

She sat up in the bog and brought Viv (eyes wide open, glazed) into her lap.

"I'm here," she said, sounding to herself like a mother in a movie, "I'm here."

"I want Mommy."

"I'm here. I'm here. I'm right here."

"I want Mommy."

"I'm here."

"I want Mommy. I want Mommy."

"I'm here!" she cried out.

"I want Mommy! I want Mommy! I want Mommy! I want Mommy!"

9

At some point Viv stopped screaming the three unbearable words. Stopped midsentence, closed her eyes and was asleep. Ben, who Molly thought had managed to sleep through Viv's frenzy, was in fact not asleep: he was watching his mother and sister, his cheek pressed against the stained sheet, perfectly still aside from the whimper she could hear only now that Viv had fallen silent.

"Little boy," Molly said to him.

His whimper escalated.

"Do you want to feel safe?" she whispered.

He looked deep into her eyes.

"Let's make a house," she said, pulling the dank bedding up over their heads so the three of them were covered. He found his way to her like a creature born in the dark, accustomed to the dark, and nuzzled his head into her stomach. She ignored the suggestion of nausea this set off within her. They could be anywhere—in a log cabin on a mountaintop, in a submarine, in a capsule floating through the universe.

She searched for his hand and found it. It was

so small. In the darkness they held hands. She could feel his heart beating in his hand.

The footsteps in the other room served as an echo of it, just another manifestation of the quick *tip-tap, tip-tap, tip-tap* of his heart. She did not believe in the footsteps as a real thing, an actual sound outside the tiny world she had created for her offspring beneath the blankets. She lay there amid her children, glistening.

No, not glistening.

Listening.

10

When Moll peeled the covers back, Ben smiled and reached for her, unperturbed by the sight of two identical mothers.

Molly would have been shocked at his reaction had she possessed any remaining energy for shock. Now that Moll was here, though, now that she had checked Moll's hands for weapons (no gun, no knife, no metal pipe), her final resources exited her body.

"Sleep," Moll said simply, and carried Ben out of the room.

And Molly could muster no resistance, no rage, only an irrepressible sensation of relief. So what if someone was taking advantage of her in her weakest moment? So what if someone was taking care of her in her weakest moment?

She rolled over toward moist, slumbering Viv, embraced her, and slept.

When she awoke, hours or days later, the sheets were clean and the bed empty of children. The sky outside was half-light, heading either toward morning or night.

She did not know how the sheets could have

been changed while she slept. It was a miracle, the explanation of which she hoped never to learn.

She stood up. Something was unsteady: the world, or herself. The thought of walking, of speaking, demolished her. Yet she managed to put on her robe and open the door and limp a few feet.

"Here's the church, here's the steeple, open the doors, see all the people!"

The children, seated at the table on either side of Moll, clapped. They were wearing clean pajamas. Their hair was wet and brushed, their fevers broken. There was food (toast, applesauce) on their plates. There was drink (neon, Gatorade) in their cups.

All three turned toward her, noticing her at the same instant.

They looked interrupted. She felt like an intruder.

Ben almost immediately turned his attention back to Moll in hopes that she would once again make her fingers into a church, a steeple, a row of people.

The children seemed vibrant, recovered.

"Hi, other Mommy," Viv said.

Terror, or nausea, swelled in Molly. She leaned against the wall.

"Are you feeling obnoxious?" Viv said.

"Obnoxious?" Distantly, Molly marveled at her daughter's big word.

316

"She means *nauseous,*" Moll said. She stood and filled a glass with Gatorade and stuck in a straw and handed it to Molly. "Go back to bed."

"Yeah," Viv added giddily. "Go back to bed!"

And because her legs refused to hold her up, she obeyed.

There was nothing she could do. There was nothing her body would allow her to do.

She was loath to admit that this was the realization of an old fantasy of hers: to be in two places at once. To have two bodies. To give herself over to her own recovery while her children were in the hands of someone who loved them exactly as she did.

But her fatigue overmastered her anguish, and she fell asleep. She slept, woke, slept, woke.

"Ready or not, here I come. Ready or not, here I come." Viv's voice, moving fast down the hallway. "Ready or not, here I come."

The six words triggered in Molly the same charge of animal fear she had always experienced during hide-and-seek, even when the seeker was just a four-year-old. Every time it was a minuscule version of hiding from men with boots and guns.

". . . or . . . not . . . here . . . I . . ." Viv wandered back up the hallway, despondent, lonely, no longer running.

"Viv!" Molly called out from the bed. "Vivian!"

But by then Moll and Ben had emerged from

317

somewhere, by then there were shrieks of surprise and laughter.

Unheeded, unneeded, Molly slept.

The scariest dream of all is the one that takes place in the room where you're sleeping.

When Moll shepherded them into their room for bedtime, Molly crept out of bed and crouched beside their door. She could hear Moll reading to them. Talking to them. *Put this on. Here you go. Yes, that's right.*

She opened the door.

Moll had claimed her spot, lodged between them on Viv's bed, nursing Ben.

Moll looked at her, startled, a criminal caught in the act. A reaction, a jolt, that she had not manifested at all when Molly had come upon her and David.

"Go away," Viv said to Molly.

"Don't say that," Moll chided.

"Well, Mommy, how about I snuggle with you for six days, and then Mommy may come in and tell me an animal story?"

11

" . . . *Now the days of David drew nigh*
that he should die;
and he charged Solomon his son,
saying,
'I go the way of all the earth: be thou
strong therefore, and shew thyself a
man;
and keep the charge of the Lord thy God,
to walk in her ways, to keep her
statutes,
and her commandments, and her judg-
ments, and her testimonies,
as it is written in the law of Moses,
that thou mayest prosper in all that thou
doest,
and withersoever thou turnest
thyself . . .' "

The familiar voice fell silent.
A steady hand on her forehead.
Just the thing she was craving.
A warm, steady hand.
Dangerous, this comfort.

Ice clinking in a glass. The fizz of ginger ale.

A figure perched on the wide windowsill, almost invisible, beneath the incomplete moon. She, too, liked to perch there, almost invisible. More than once she had frightened David when he entered the bedroom, believing it empty.

Now, lined up on the windowsill: a Coca-Cola bottle, an Altoids tin, a toy soldier, a potsherd, a penny.

"Then came there two women, that were
	harlots, unto the king,
and stood before him.
And the one woman said,
'O my lord, I and this woman dwell in
	one house;
and I was delivered of a child with her in
	the house.
And it came to pass the third day after
	that I was delivered,
that this woman was delivered also:
and we were together; there was no
	stranger with us in the house,
save we two in the house.
And this woman's child died in the night;
	because she overlaid it.
And she arose at midnight,
and took my son from beside me, while
	thine handmaid slept,
and laid it in her bosom,

and laid her dead child in my bosom.
And when I rose in the morning to give
    my child suck,
behold, it was dead:
but when I had considered it in the
    morning,
behold, it was not my son, which I did
    bear.'
And the other woman said,
'Nay; but the living is my son, and the
    dead is thy son.'
And this said,
'No; but the dead is thy son, and the
    living is my son.'
Thus they spake before the king. Then
    said the king,
'The one saith, This is my son that liveth,
    and thy son is the dead:
and the other saith, Nay; but thy son is
    the dead, and my son is the living.'
And the king said, 'Bring me a sword.'
And they brought a sword before the
    king.
And the king said, 'Divide the living
    child in two,
and give half to the one,
and half to the other.'
Then spake the woman whose the living
    child was unto the king,
for her bowels yearned upon her son,

and she said,
'O my lord, give her the living child, and
in no wise slay it.'
But the other said,
'Let it be neither mine nor thine, but
divide it.'
Then the king answered and said,
'Give her the living child, and in no wise
slay it:
she is the mother thereof.' "

The two women and their single shadow left the palace on a street paved with gold. They walked until the gold turned to dirt, and they kept walking. The road was long and straight. No sound but the sound of pebbles shifting beneath their feet. Sometimes one would carry the baby. Sometimes the other would carry the baby. They did not have water or anything else. They walked. They were two women with one live child and one ghost child. They were two women with four children. They were three women with six children, nine women with eighteen children, fifty women with a hundred children, five hundred women with a thousand children, their single shadow before them.

12

Moll closed the Bible and placed it on the windowsill beside her, between the Coca-Cola bottle and the Altoids tin.

"That should be destroyed," Molly said from the bed, her mouth sour from sickness. Sadness rippled through her at the thought of obliterating the Bible. But presumably there was, somewhere, a world containing many thousands of copies of it.

"So," Moll said, "you agree with her."

"Her?"

"The bomber."

"What?"

"She, too, wanted to destroy the Bible."

Molly struggled to sit up in bed. She felt weak, dehydrated, uncertain of her abilities.

"Can you," Moll continued, "imagine any circumstance under which you could do what she did?"

"No!" Molly said.

She looked at Moll and Moll looked at her.

"Only," Molly admitted, "if. The children."

It was true, she knew it, she could feel it solid

within her, she bore inside herself all the dark possibilities: she would hide and lie and steal and starve and plot and be merciless and insinuate herself into someone else's life. She would kill and she would die. If.

"Where is she now?" Molly said. "The one in this world, the one who . . . didn't." She pictured her crouching in every shadow, lingering behind every tree.

"Who knows," Moll said.

And Molly saw her: running through a parking lot, crying at a bus stop, drinking desperately from a water fountain.

"The thing about that woman," Moll said, very quietly. "The bomber. She." Moll paused. "She really looked a lot like us."

13

"Are you okay?"

"Well, I'm dizzy."

Dizziness was one word for it: this sense of increasing distance from the known facts of her own life.

Billions of Mollies in billions of universes. Billions of Davids. All those other Vivs and Bens, their voices echoing through infinity, their eyes multiplied across the void like stars.

"Me too."

Molly considered the Molly before her: a slight woman perched on a windowsill. This person was her nemesis, yet the sight of Moll inspired only a strange sense of calm.

She found herself thinking of the Pit, vaguely sodden at the bottom, its innocuous smell of dust and water.

"E pluribus unum," Moll said.

"What?"

Moll picked up the penny off the windowsill and carried it to the bed and dropped it into Molly's palm. It was surprisingly warm, almost searing, and Molly understood that it burned with its otherworldliness, until she remembered that the radiator beneath the windowsill had turned on for the evening.

Moll returned to the windowsill and closed her eyes.

Molly, too, closed her eyes, wondering what Moll saw on the inside of her lids.

Two parents form a circle around two small naked children.

"The umbilical cord," Moll said, "runs both directions. The mother keeps the children alive and the children keep the mother alive."

Molly opened her eyes. Moll's were still closed.

"Whenever I'm playing with them," Moll said, "I'm grieving them."

Then Moll opened her eyes and made a gesture with her hand, a sort of flicking away of the words.

Molly knew she would never forget that hopeless gesture of Moll's hand.

Moll, who belonged nowhere.

Molly, who did now sometimes grieve them when she was playing with them, but not always.

On the windowsill, the Coca-Cola bottle glimmered with its own light, and the toy soldier fluttered its monkey tail.

"Come here," Molly said, but Moll stayed on the windowsill.

"It's always going to be a duel," Moll said.

Or maybe she said, "It's always going to be a dual."

At last Moll came down off the windowsill. Stepped across the room to Molly and lay down beside her on the bed and took her hand.

"My palm is sweaty."

"Mine too."

"Well, yes."

Moll placed her other hand on Molly's forehead. Again, the perfect steadiness.

"Fever's broken."

Molly knew that it was, but she did not want Moll to remove her hand, and when Moll did, she suffered a minor sensation of bereavement.

They lay side by side, holding hands.

And then Moll was on top of her, Moll's face so close to her face. Their identical arms met, elbow to elbow. There was a moment when Molly could have thrown her off, could have asked indignantly what the hell Moll was doing, but that moment passed. She matched her shoulders to her shoulders. Her feet to her feet. Her thighs to her thighs. Her forehead to her forehead. Lungs to lungs, womb to womb, teeth to teeth.

She pressed down on her as though trying to press past her skin, into her blood, her muscles, her bones.

The sublime pressure.

It felt good, she had to admit, so good, until all at once it became too much, far too much to bear.

— Epilogue —

She woke, new.

The morning bright and quiet.

When her feet touched the floor beside the bed, an intense vitality surged through her legs.

This superhuman strength carried her down the hallway to the place where they slept. She opened the door and every single bit of love she had accumulated for them over the months and years was present in the room, or was the room.

After watching them sleep for some minutes, she went to the hall closet to get the backpack. She filled it with the necessary things: the diapers, the wipes, the apples, the string cheese, the crackers, the nuts, the water bottle, the sunscreen, the hats, the charger, the tablets, the first-aid kit, the Coca-Cola bottle, the toy soldier, the Altoids tin, the potsherd, the penny. The Bible.

On her phone, there was a text from him, a cheeky tender pair of sentences sent just before dawn, and, abundant with love, she replied in kind.

The moment had arrived to awaken them into the renewed happiness of the home. Recognizing it, they were happy too, and ate well, drank well, were amenable to the application of sunscreen. The baby took the milk he needed from her, rich, dripping white as he laughed.

When she went to the bathroom, leaving them alone together on the rug for a moment, she overheard the girl saying to the boy: "How could you be such cuter?"

She donned the backpack and opened the front door, the children pressing behind her. Holding the girl's hand, carrying the boy effortlessly on her hip, she walked up and down the blocks in the surprising heat, searching for the car.

But she could not find it anywhere. She had no memory of parking it. All the blocks blurred into one.

They went back home and got the stroller, the baby carrier. She strapped the baby to her. She snapped the girl into the stroller. The children were agreeable, curious.

She could do the miles, even in this heat. She was in awe of her vigor, her rigor.

That familiar old slog of marching somewhere with both, pushing the kid in the stroller while the baby grows ever sweatier, ever heavier, against your chest, the diaper full. Today, though, her energies doubled, she could more than handle it. She did not ache. She moved quickly, despite her burdens. She was hyperaware of her thighs, her calves, the power with which they propelled her and the children across the pavement.

To any passerby she would have looked like any mother out for a walk with her kids.

The sun warned of the summer to come. She had forgotten her sunglasses. But her eyes were tougher now.

Every so often her hands searched for their wrists, their pulses at first evading her fingertips, then found.

There was a moment when a fire truck came down the frontage road, heading straight toward them, wailing and flashing, before turning left.

But the children were not alarmed, for they were with her, safe, and she bore them onward.

Acknowledgments

It brings me joy to acknowledge:

Sarah E. Allen, for her awe-inspiring expertise in paleobotany. Vanessa Monson, for sharing her knowledge of archaeology. Lisa Schwebel, for consultation about Biblical matters. Nora Lisman Zimbler, for our conversations about psychology and loss.

My agent, Faye Bender, whose steady heart and hand have guided me for so many years now. Jenny Meyer and Jason Richman, for supporting this book.

My editor, Marysue Rucci, whose exceptional passion and brilliance have enabled this book to become more fully itself. Zachary Knoll, for his acumen and attention to detail. Jonathan Karp, for his powerful advocacy. The rest of the Simon & Schuster team, especially Elizabeth Breeden, Toi Crockett, Erica Ferguson, Alison Forner, Christine Foye, Cary Goldstein, Kayley Hoffman, Amanda Lang, David Litman, Heidi Meier, Tracy Nelson, Lewelin Polanco, Carolyn Reidy, Richard Rhorer, Wendy Sheanin, and Gary Urda. My editor Poppy Hampson at

Chatto & Windus, for her keen and caring eye.

All of those many friends who have provided insight along the way, literary and otherwise, with special thanks to my generous early readers: Sarah Baron, Amelia Kahaney, Elizabeth Logan Harris, and Maisie Tivnan. And to Laura Perciasepe for the sound advice.

My colleagues and teachers, current and former, in the Brooklyn College Department of English, with special thanks to Joshua Henkin, Jenny Offill, Ellen Tremper, and Mac Wellman.

My students, who have graced my classrooms and my life with their curiosity and energy.

The CUNY Office of Research for the CUNY Book Completion Award.

David Barry, for the photographs.

The editors of my previous books: Sarah Bowlin, Lisa Graziano, and Krista Marino.

My wonderful family, with special thanks to my mother-in-law, Gail Thompson, for plot advice and for excelling at grandparent duty, along with my father-in-law, Doug Thompson. My grandparents, Paul Phillips, Sr., and Mary Jane Zimmermann. My brother, Mark Phillips, for talking science-fiction portals with me. My sister Alice Light, always my earliest reader. My father, Paul Phillips, Jr., for his lifelong encouragement.

My husband, Adam Douglas Thompson, my collaborator in all things great and small.

My beloved daughter and my beloved son.

My mother, Susan Zimmermann, and my sister Katherine Rose Phillips, to whom this book is dedicated.

ABOUT THE AUTHOR

HELEN PHILLIPS is the author of five books, including the collection *Some Possible Solutions*, which received the 2017 John Gardner Fiction Book Award. Her novel *The Beautiful Bureaucrat*, a *New York Times* Notable Book of 2015, was a finalist for the Los Angeles Times Book Prize and the New York Public Library Young Lions Award. Her collection *And Yet They Were Happy* was named a notable collection by The Story Prize. Helen has received a Rona Jaffe Foundation Writers' Award and the Calvino Prize in fabulist fiction. Her work has appeared in *The Atlantic*, the *New York Times*, and *Tin House*, and on *Selected Shorts*. She is an associate professor at Brooklyn College and lives in Brooklyn with her husband, artist Adam Douglas Thompson, and their children. Visit HelenCPhillips.com.

Center Point Large Print
600 Brooks Road / PO Box 1
Thorndike, ME 04986-0001 USA

(207) 568-3717

US & Canada:
1 800 929-9108
www.centerpointlargeprint.com